JACK B. QUICK
Sports Detective

THE WORLD'S SMARTEST SPORTS DETECTIVE!

THE CASE OF THE "MISSING" PLAYBOOK
and other mysteries

D1111803

By L. E. Wolfe

A *SPORTS ILLUSTRATED FOR KIDS* BOOK

The Case of the "Missing" Playbook by K. B. Gardner/Bill Gutman.
The Case of the Wiped-out Windsurfer by Ian McMahan.
The Case of the Unset Nets by Jon Pearce.
The Case of the Lucky Lady by Bill Gutman.
Cover art by Paul Kirchner. Cover design by Martha Sedgewick.
Creative consultation by L. E. Wolfe.
Produced by Angel Entertainment, Inc.

SPORTS ILLUSTRATED FOR KIDS is a trademark of THE TIME INC. MAGAZINE
COMPANY

SPORTS ILLUSTRATED FOR KIDS Books is a joint imprint of Little, Brown and
Company and Warner Juvenile Books.

Printed in the United States of America

First Printing: October 1990
10 9 8 7 6 5 4 3 2 1

Published simultaneously in Canada by Little, Brown & Company (Canada) Limited

Library of Congress Cataloging-in-Publication Data
Wolfe, L. E., 1961—
        The case of the "missing" playbook : and other mysteries / by L. E. Wolfe.
            p.   cm.— (Jack B. Quick, sports detective ; #2)
        "A Sports illustrated for kids book."
        Summary: Twelve-year-old Jack B. Quick and his friends investigate a suspicious
        football defeat and three other sports-related mysteries.
        ISBN 0-316-72911-6 (pbk.)
        [1. Sports—Fiction. 2. Mystery and detective stories.]
I. Title. II. Title : Case of the "missing" playbook. III. Series.
PZ.W8185533Cas   1990   90-50343
[Fic]—dc20   CIP
                                                                                AC

Contents

The Case of the "Missing" Playbook

"Let's go, Vikings!" Nina Chin yelled at the top of her lungs. She shook her head and turned toward me, her long black braid swinging over her shoulder. "Jack, it doesn't look good for us, does it?"

I had to agree with Nina. It didn't seem as if the Central Vikings were going to be able to win this game. Nina and I were sitting with Ollie Steele in the middle of the bleachers surrounded by black and gold, the Viking colors.

This game was turning out to be a major disappointment. It was the division championship and the winner would go to the county championship. I had been looking forward to a great matchup because Central was undefeated this year and Roosevelt had not lost any games either. But it was turning out to be one uneven ball game. At the start of the fourth quarter, Central was behind by 15 points.

"Maybe we'll get something going now," Ollie said hopefully. Ollie's cousin, Wells Douglas, is Central's star running back and free safety. He is also one of Central's co-captains. Ollie idolizes his cousin, and he can't wait to get into high school and play for the Vikings, just like Wells. Even though they are cousins, they look more like brothers. They even have the same haircut: a high-top fade.

We leaned forward as Central came to the line of scrimmage. The Vikings had fought their way to the Roosevelt 37-yard line and quarterback Tom Parsons got set to call the signals on an important third-down play.

Ollie nudged me excitedly. "I bet they're going to try a reverse," he said. "You see how Johnson is a step behind the line?" he asked, pointing to Central's wide receiver, Eric Johnson. "Wells told me that when Johnson does that, it means he's going to come back for the ball."

Since Ollie and Wells are so close, Ollie knows the Vikings' formations backward and forward.

"Whatever it is, I hope it works," Nina said with an anxious expression on her face. "We're running out of time."

"The reverse almost always works," Ollie replied. "The opposing team usually doesn't expect it, and it hasn't been run at all today. This should be just the big gainer the Vikings need."

We could hear Parsons calling the signals, although his voice was hoarse. At the snap, he gave the ball to Wells, who appeared to be running a sweep to the left. But as he passed Johnson, Wells gave the ball to him. Johnson, who is the fastest player on the team, took it going full stride and began to run toward the right sideline. All three of us jumped to our feet screaming.

"All right!" Ollie yelled. "Way to go, Wells. C'mon—"

But before the words were out of Ollie's mouth, the play ended. Roosevelt's left defensive end and left outside linebacker had come up quickly and were waiting for Johnson before he could even turn up the sideline. Johnson was knocked to the ground and the play lost eight yards.

"This is a total nightmare!" Nina exclaimed, sitting back down on the bleachers with a stunned expression.

Ollie didn't say a thing. He just stood there, shaking his head in disbelief.

I couldn't believe it myself. The Vikings had fielded just about their best football team ever. Coming into this game with the Roosevelt Tigers, they had an 8-0 record. They had even been considered a 10-point favorite over the 7-1 Tigers.

I had really expected to see Central win its first division championship in 12 years. Instead, the Vikings were losing by more than two touchdowns. I guess it really just goes to show that in sports you never know what's going to happen. And I should know that because I'm a sports detective. My name is Jack B. Quick. Ollie and Nina are my associates.

A few minutes later, the Tigers had the ball at the Viking 41-yard line, and it was third down and long.

"This could be a major play!" Ollie exclaimed excitedly, grabbing my arm. "If we stop them now, we might still be able to get back in the game." He studied the field intently. "Watch Wells," he continued. "If he moves closer to the middle, then he's probably going to blitz."

As the Tiger quarterback stood over center, I noticed

that Wells *did* seem closer to the middle of the formation than he usually did at his free safety position. I knew that the Vikings sometimes blitzed when they were expecting a pass play.

Wells' voice carried to the top of the bleachers as he called out "Blue Diamond!" I figured that Blue Diamond must be the Vikings' code name for a blitz. All the plays in a football playbook have code names. That way, when a team steps up to the line of scrimmage and sees the opposing team's formation, the players can decide on a new play right on the field without anyone else knowing what they're doing.

The Tiger center snapped the ball sharply. The quarterback dropped back for the pass.

"Sack him, Wells!" Ollie screamed, jumping up.

Wells and the rest of the defensive line rushed forward and tried to tackle the quarterback for a loss before he could unload the ball. Only it didn't work. The quarterback took two quick steps forward and fired a bullet over the blitzing players. His split end caught the ball at the line of scrimmage, and then pivoted, cut to the right side and charged up the sideline toward the end zone. The Viking strong safety didn't have a prayer of catching him.

"I don't believe it!" Ollie exclaimed. "That was the perfect way to beat the blitz. It's like they knew it was coming!"

"And Roosevelt's been doing that all afternoon!" Nina added. "It's almost as if the players have E.S.P."

"Well, the Vikings are just not on today," Ollie admitted. "The Tiger coach, Max Devitt, must have done a good job of scouting the Vikings."

Great scouting or not, I thought there was still something a little strange about the fact that the Vikings couldn't get anything going. And that didn't change as the final minutes ticked away. The game ended with the Tigers winning 29-7.

Our side of the stands was pretty quiet as the crowd got to its feet and started filing down the bleacher steps.

"You'd never know the Vikings were undefeated from what happened out there today," Nina said dejectedly, as we trooped down to the field.

We walked over to the Viking bench. Most of the players had already headed into the gym, but Wells was still there. He was sitting on the end of the bench, his head down.

"Hey, Wells," Ollie called to his cousin as we walked up behind the depressed player.

Wells looked up and tried to smile at his younger cousin. The smile turned out more like a grimace, though. "Hi, Ol," he greeted Ollie softly. "Sorry we didn't give you much to cheer about today."

"What happened out there?" Nina asked bluntly. Nina is one of those people who always gets right to the point.

Wells turned to look at her and shrugged. "I don't know," he admitted. "It was like they were inside our jerseys all day. They might as well have had a copy of our playbook." He shrugged again and stood up. "I'm sorry," he apologized once again. Then Wells followed his teammates toward the locker room.

Ollie watched him go for a moment. I knew it was hard on him to see his favorite cousin so depressed. "Wells is right," Ollie said, turning to face Nina and me. "The Tigers played as if they were inside the Viking uniforms. Maybe they *do* have E.S.P." He scuffed his sneaker into the dirt and stared down at the ground.

"They sure knew everything the Vikings were going to do," Nina agreed.

"Come on," I said, trying to bring my friends back to reality. I mean, I was upset we had lost . . . but E.S.P.? No way. "That's impossible," I declared firmly. Neither of them looked convinced.

"Well, how else can you explain it?" Nina asked me.

I couldn't. Then, something occurred to me. "Just a second!" I exclaimed. "What was it that Wells told us about the Tigers having a playbook?"

"He wasn't serious," Ollie replied. "It would be close to impossible for anyone on Roosevelt's team to get a hold of one of our playbooks. They all guard their copies with their lives."

"But if a playbook somehow got into the hands of the Tigers, they would know all the signals and formations, wouldn't they?" Nina asked Ollie.

"Definitely," Ollie replied and then frowned. "But that wouldn't happen. There's no way they could get a playbook. And even if they did, there would be no way we could ever prove it."

Although I, too, was still unconvinced, my mind started whirling just thinking about the possibility. It would have been one thing if the Tigers had thwarted a couple of the Viking plays here and there. But they had done it all afternoon.

"Let's go to Kreagle's for ice cream," Nina suggested. Ollie and I agreed, and after we'd gotten our bikes from the rack in front of the high school, we pedaled over.

"You know," I began, after we sat down at the counter in Kreagle's, "if Roosevelt had one of our playbooks, it would explain a lot of things."

"It sure would," Nina agreed, swiveling her stool to face me. "But Ollie says it would be impossible for another school to get a copy of one."

"It definitely would be," Ollie insisted again after we had ordered our ice cream cones. "Besides, I can't imagine any coach would want to win that way. I mean, that's outright cheating!"

"But Coach Devitt isn't just any coach," Nina pointed out. "He wants to win at any cost. You know that old saying, 'Winning's not everything—it's the *only* thing.' Well, I think Coach Devitt *wrote* that!"

Even though the saying is usually associated with former Green Bay Packer coach Vince Lombardi, we could not rule out the idea that Coach Devitt might stoop that low to win. And the more I thought about the possibility of Roosevelt having a copy of Central's playbook, the more all those thwarted plays made sense. Central was too good a team to mess up that much—without a reason.

"Jack B. Quick," Ollie said, breaking into my thoughts. "I know that look. It's your we're-about-to-start-investigating-something look. I hope it's not this playbook thing."

Luckily, the arrival of our ice cream distracted him momentarily.

"Why not?" I asked after a few licks of my chocolate fudge cone.

"Because it would be a waste of time," Ollie said heatedly. "Stuff like that just doesn't happen. . . ."

"Hold on, Ol," I said, cutting him off. "Just for a second, imagine what a game would be like if one of the teams had gotten its hands on the other team's playbook."

Ollie shook his head, as if he didn't even want to consider the possibility. "Well," he finally began, "the team with the playbook would blow the other team off the field."

"Like the Tigers did to the Vikings this afternoon, right?" I asked, pushing my glasses up on my nose and taking a deep breath. "You see, Ollie, no matter what you may want to believe, it's a definite possibility. I think we should go back over to Central and talk to Coach Marsh. Are you both coming with me?"

Δ   Δ   Δ

By the time we got back to the high school, most of the players had already showered and were out of the locker room. Roger Marsh was still in his office, however. The only problem was that someone was with him.

"Oh, no!" Nina exclaimed, as soon as she realized who that someone was. "It's Milo Martin!"

Ollie groaned. "Now we'll never get a chance to talk to the coach."

Milo Martin is the top reporter for the Johnson Junior

High newspaper, *The Eagle*. He wants to be an investigative reporter when he grows up, and he's certainly getting his feet wet on *The Eagle*. Milo and I have crossed each other's paths before. It isn't surprising, considering that he wants to be an *investigative* reporter and that I am an investigator. Even though I think he's a major pain, I have to admit that he is a good reporter.

"I think we should go wait by the lockers around the corner," I said quickly. It sounded as if Milo and the coach were just finishing up their interview. "We wouldn't want Milo to know that we might have a case. It could blow the whole thing before we even get started."

We ducked behind the bank of lockers just as Milo stepped into the locker room. "Thanks, Coach," Milo said. "I'm sorry about the game."

We waited until we heard the locker room door shut and then walked back to Coach Marsh's office. I knocked on the open door, and then we stepped into the office.

The coach looked up. "Can I help you?" he asked wearily.

"Hi," I said, moving forward to shake Coach Marsh's hand. "My name is Jack B. Quick and these are my associates, Nina Chin and Ollie Steele."

Standing slowly, the coach extended his hand. He had a very firm grasp. "The sports detective," he said as though he had heard of me. "What can I do for you?"

"Well . . . " I began, hesitating for a second. I hoped our theory wouldn't sound too far-fetched to the coach. It had seemed perfectly reasonable at Kreagle's. "We think that maybe there's a reason that Roosevelt stomped all over us on the field today."

"Yeah?" the coach asked frowning. "*I* can tell you why."

I took a step forward. Did the coach already suspect something about the playbook?

"They had the better team today," Coach Marsh continued sharply. "And we played very badly." He frowned, deep lines furrowing his forehead.

"That's not what we meant," Nina cut in. "We think someone on the Tiger team got his hands on one of your playbooks."

I sighed. Blunt as usual, Nina had dropped that information like a ton of bricks. I knew from experience that sometimes it's better to break shocking news gently to people. I sat down and quickly outlined our theory before the coach could object. The coach kept shaking his head.

"There's no way!" he exclaimed when I finished speaking. "They couldn't have gotten a playbook. My boys would never lose one. And they'd absolutely tell me if they had. You ought to know that," Coach Marsh said, looking over at Ollie. "Isn't Wells Douglas your cousin?"

Ollie nodded. "Yeah, but I think Jack may be right. The Vikings are too good to get their doors blown off the way they did today."

The coach leaned back in his chair, as if suddenly struck by a major thought. "You know, I really can't understand why they ran all over us today," he murmured to himself. "But I did have this strange feeling that Max Devitt was reading my mind. He was ready for everything I threw at him."

I could see that he was now considering our playbook theory. "We'd like to investigate the possibility," I said to the coach.

Coach Marsh hesitated. "Now listen, I don't want anyone thinking we're sore losers. We may have lost, fair and square," he began. "In fact, it's much more likely that we just had a bad day—a terrible day."

"We're very discreet," Nina cut in. "No one needs to know that we've even talked to you about our theory. Let's just say we're curious."

"I don't know . . . " the coach said slowly. I could tell that we had him now. "I guess if you were discreet . . ."

Score! I thought.

"When will you know if anyone's missing a playbook?" Ollie asked, getting right into the investigation.

"I'm collecting the playbooks at our last team meeting on Monday," Coach Marsh replied. "I'll know then."

"Do you also have extra copies of the playbook, Coach?" Nina asked.

"Sure, I keep a couple of extra copies in my desk," he said.

"O.K., we'll stop by after your meeting," I said, standing up. We all shook the coach's hand and told him we'd be in touch if we found out anything important in the meantime.

We walked outside into the early evening. There was a chill in the autumn air as we set out to solve what I had come to think of as *The Case of the Missing Playbook*.

JACK B. QUICK

Early the next morning, I was in my "office," which is actually my driveway, shooting baskets. For some reason, I always think better when I'm shooting hoops.

The night before when I'd gotten back from the high school, I had labeled a floppy disk *The Case of the "Missing" Playbook* and started a new file. I decided to put the word missing in quotes because we didn't know whether the playbook had actually changed hands. Unfortunately, there wasn't anything in the file yet except the date, the score of the game and Coach Marsh's name. I hoped that we could get something going soon.

"Hey, Jack!" Ollie called out as he walked up my driveway.

"Hi, Ollie," I replied, carefully taking aim for a three-pointer. The ball sailed in a high arc toward the basket, hit the rim and bounced out. Ollie jogged in and grabbed the rebound.

"I thought I should get over here early today," Ollie said. "We really don't have much to go on with this case. We're going to need all the time we can get."

"You're right," I agreed. I had a feeling this was going to be a tough case—maybe our toughest ever. Especially since we didn't even have any evidence that there *was* a case. "You know, Ollie . . . " I began, and then paused. "Do you think it's possible that someone *gave* a Viking playbook to the Tigers?"

Ollie turned to look at me just as he took a shot. I noticed that the ball swished through the net without even touching the rim. "You mean, you think one of the Vikings

12

is a traitor, and helped the Tigers blow them out yesterday?!"
Ollie exclaimed. "You think someone would *purposely* ruin
an undefeated season?"

"I don't know," I said with a shrug, trying to sound
calm. Ollie sometimes gets pretty worked up over things.
"But it's a possibility, don't you think? I mean, if a player
lost his playbook, he would have told the coach, wouldn't
he?" So if the Tigers had lucked into the lost book, at least
Coach Marsh would have known that someone else might
have seen the plays.

Ollie dribbled for a few minutes without looking up. "I
guess you're right," he finally admitted. "Maybe we should
go talk to Wells."

"That's a great idea!" I exclaimed. "Let's go!"

Wells was out mowing his front lawn when we got to
his house. As soon as he caught sight of us, he cut the engine.
"What's up, guys?" he asked, wiping the sweat off his face
with the bottom of his T-shirt. The day was surprisingly
warm for late autumn.

"Hi, Wells," Ollie said. "How's it going?"

"Well, I'll live," Wells replied with a faint smile.

"Listen, Wells," I began. I kind of wished Nina was
with us so she could just blurt out our theory. Sometimes
bluntness has its place. "We . . . um . . . we kind of have this
theory based on something you said."

"Something I said?" Wells asked. "What? When?"

"After the game yesterday," Ollie began, "you said that
the Tigers played like they were in your jerseys."

"Oh, yeah," Wells replied. "What about it?"

I explained our theory to him. As I spoke, he kept shaking his head. "No way, Jack," he said when I was finished. "No one lost a playbook. I mean, I'd know. I'm one of the captains. Someone would have told me. But thanks for trying, guys. We lost. What can I say?"

"Well, what if one of the Vikings gave a copy of his playbook to someone on the Roosevelt team?" I asked. "Come on, Wells. It was like the Tigers were psychic or something. They seemed to know every play you called— *before* you called it. They were ready for everything. I don't believe it was all just dumb luck."

"Jack, I'm sorry, but I don't see it," Wells said, still shaking his head. "We had an undefeated season. No one would mess that up on purpose."

"But Wells . . . " Ollie began. "The Vikings are too good to get pounded like that. Something was definitely up."

"Would a playbook be hard to copy?" I asked Wells.

Wells thought for a second. "Not really," he replied. "They're just loose-leaf notebooks, so it'd be easy to take out some or all of the pages, copy them and then put them back in."

I exchanged glances with Ollie.

"You know," Wells continued, "I'm not totally buying into this copied playbook theory, but you *might* have something." He frowned. "I don't know if this means anything, but last week Bobby Richards was kidding around—only I don't think he was really kidding—and he tossed his playbook into the trash can. He said since he never played, he didn't need it anymore."

"Bobby Richards is Central High's second string quarterback, right?" Ollie asked his cousin.

"Yeah," Wells answered. He shifted his weight from one foot to the other. I could tell that he was uncomfortable talking about any of his teammates behind their backs.

"Well . . . Bobby really wanted to play all year. In fact, he felt he *should* have played. And he let everyone know that."

"So maybe Bobby felt that if he gave a playbook to the Tigers and they got enough of a lead, the coach would make some changes in the lineup," I said thoughtfully. "Like, for instance, bring in a new quarterback."

"But why would he even allow Roosevelt to get a lead?" Ollie asked, confused. "There would be no guarantee that Bobby could get it back."

"That's true," I said, "but we should probably check him out, anyway." I turned to Wells. "Thanks for your help," I said. It wasn't much, but at least it gave us a place to start.

Wells nodded. "Let me know if you find anything out, O.K.?" he said, as he bent down to restart the mower's engine.

Ollie and I headed down Wells' driveway. We had to find Bobby Richards right away.

"Hey, guys!" Wells suddenly called, cutting the engine. "I just thought of something else. Coach Marsh and Todd Donlin were having a major shouting match yesterday before the game. I have no clue what it was all about, though."

"Who's Todd Donlin?" I asked.

Wells told us that Todd had been the Viking fullback five years earlier. He had gone to college for a couple of years, but then dropped out. He had been hanging around the team all season, trying to convince Coach Marsh to hire him as an assistant. But the coach wouldn't do it. Wells had heard through the grapevine that when Todd had played for Central, he had sometimes acted as if he knew more than the coaches did. Coach Marsh obviously did not want that kind of attitude passed on to his team. Maybe Todd was looking for a way to make Central and its coach look bad on the field.

Ollie and I thanked Wells again, hopped on our bikes and headed down the street. Now we had two suspects. Not too bad for an hour's work.

Δ   Δ   Δ

Early that afternoon, Nina joined Ollie and me, and the three of us headed over to Kramer's department store. Bobby Richards worked there part-time as a stockboy on Sundays. We got there just as Bobby was starting his lunch break. There is nothing like good timing.

"Bobby Richards?" I asked the dark-haired, muscular boy who was sitting on the loading dock around back. He was eating a huge roast beef sandwich.

"Yeah," he answered without looking up. "What do you want?"

"I'm Jack B. Quick," I said and paused, waiting for him to look up. After he did, I continued. "And these are my associates, Nina Chin and Ollie Steele. Can we talk to you for a minute?"

"Jack B. Quick," Bobby repeated. "Aren't you that

sports detective people are always talking about?"

I nodded. "We're just checking into the possibility that there may be a specific and unethical reason why the Vikings lost to the Tigers by so much yesterday."

"Come on, Quick," Bobby said, taking a bite out of his sandwich. "The season's over. Let it lie."

"Well, we think the Tigers may have gotten one of your playbooks," Nina said.

"What?!" Bobby exclaimed, looking a little shocked. "How could they get one of our playbooks?"

"That's what we're trying to find out," Ollie said. "We thought maybe you could help. I mean, weren't you surprised how the Tigers totally outplayed you?"

"I guess they just had a good day," Bobby replied with a shrug. "And we had a lousy one. Of course, Coach could have made some changes—like putting me in when Parsons couldn't get a thing going. I even told him that."

It was obvious to me that Bobby Richards didn't really care whether or not Roosevelt had a Central playbook. The only thing he was upset about was the fact that he hadn't played. I tried again and asked him if he had heard anything about a misplaced playbook or one that was copied.

"It couldn't happen," Bobby said and then paused. He frowned and glared at me suddenly. "You don't think *I* had anything to do with this theory of yours, do you? Because you can just forget about it. My playbook is at home, and you can check with the coach when I turn it in tomorrow."

Ollie hurried to assure Bobby that we were not trying to implicate him in anything. But I wasn't so sure. I mean, just because he had the playbook didn't mean anything. He could have given the Tigers a copy of it, no problem.

"If you ask me, Roosevelt was just better prepared," Bobby said, stopping us as we were about to walk away. "Coach Devitt and some of his players were scouting us out at our game last week."

Ollie, Nina and I just stood there staring at him.

"Anyway," Bobby continued, "Coach Devitt even went into Coach Marsh's office after the game two weeks ago and told him to his face that the Tigers were going to humiliate us." He took a long swallow of lemonade. "I guess he was right."

"Coach Devitt was in the coach's office at Central?" Nina asked with surprise. I could tell exactly where she was leading with that question. It meant that Coach Devitt had actually been in the same office where extra copies of the playbook were kept.

"Sure," Bobby answered, unconcerned. "He and Coach Marsh are old rivals. They get like this every season. Devitt likes to win—what can I say?"

I wondered just how far Coach Devitt would really go to win a game over his long-time rival. But I didn't think Bobby could answer that question. We thanked him for his help and walked away. Now we had three suspects.

Δ   Δ   Δ

After dinner the following night, I was outside in my office dribbling a basketball and trying to sort through the case. As planned, Ollie, Nina and I had stopped in to see Coach Marsh after his players had turned in their playbooks.

There wasn't much in the way of new information. Every player had turned in a playbook. The next day, Ollie and I would head over to talk to Todd, the guy who wanted desperately to be an assistant coach.

I was working on my left-handed layup when Ollie skidded to a stop behind me. "Hey, Jack!" he called, getting off his bike. "Guess what I found out?"

"What?" I asked, pausing mid-drive.

"There's a guy on my basketball team, Joey Frank," Ollie said. "His brother Marty is a tackle for the Vikings. Maybe you've heard of him—he was All-County tackle last season."

"Oh, yeah," I replied. "I remember reading about him and T.J. Hardy, the Viking who was a shoo-in for All-County guard. The article said that they were probably the best guard-tackle tandem in the county—ever." I remembered the head shots that had accompanied the article, too. Marty looked like a big, tough guy, but he had a wide smile on his face and his eyes were all crinkled up as if he was laughing at something. T.J.'s pimply face was scowling fiercely at the camera—like he was ready to bite someone's head off. Talk about different personalities.

"Yup, that's him," Ollie said. "Joey says he overheard Marty talking to their dad after the game. Marty was complaining that he didn't think T.J. played with his usual intensity, almost as if he didn't care whether the Vikings won or lost."

"But I saw T.J. slam his helmet on the ground when the game ended," I said. "He sure wasn't acting as if he didn't care then," I told Ollie, feeling a little confused.

"I remember," Ollie replied. "I'm just telling you what Joey told me."

"Well, it's probably worth looking into," I said. "We don't really have that much else to go on at this point."

We said goodnight and made plans to meet right after school the next day to go talk to Todd Donlin. I thought I would send Nina to talk to Marty and if she had time, maybe to T.J. too. I had a hunch that Todd was going to be a tough nut to crack.

Δ   Δ   Δ

On Tuesday afternoon, Ollie and I found Todd up to his elbows in a car engine. He worked at L & J Auto Repair as a mechanic.

"Todd Donlin?" Ollie asked, careful not to brush against anything greasy.

Todd looked up. "What can I do for you kids?" he asked without taking his hands out of the engine. "You need a tricycle fixed or something?" He laughed at his own joke.

"Actually," I said, "my name is Jack B. Quick, and this is my associate, Ollie Steele. We're looking into the Viking loss to the Tigers on Saturday. Were you at the game?"

"Sure," Todd replied. "I go to all the games. I used to play for Central."

"We know," Ollie said. "You started at fullback for two years."

Todd looked surprised and a little pleased. Maybe now he would take us more seriously. "That's right," he said.

"And you want to coach for them now, right?" I asked.

20

Straightening up, Todd reached for a rag to wipe his hands. "That's right," he repeated. "But I suppose you know that Marsh doesn't want me."

Ollie and I nodded.

"It's too bad," Todd continued. "I could really help the backs. My last year playing was Coach Marsh's first year coaching. He didn't understand the fullback position, and things always had to be done his way. He still doesn't know about backs, and he won't let me help him. I'll get my chance someday, though, and I'll show him."

Todd stopped himself, as if suddenly aware that he had an audience.

"Todd, we suspect that a copy of a Viking playbook got passed along to the Tigers before the game on Saturday," I said.

Todd looked a little taken aback, but I couldn't tell if it was because he didn't believe a playbook had actually been stolen or because someone had figured out that a "missing" Central playbook had ended up with Roosevelt.

"Well, if that happened," Todd began doubtfully, "Marsh is to blame. The coach should know where every playbook is at all times."

"But how would Marsh know if someone had copied a playbook?" Ollie asked, stepping closer to the car on which Todd was working. Now that Ollie was involved in questioning a suspect, it was clear that getting a little grease on himself was the last thing on his mind.

"Listen," Todd said sharply. "I don't have anything to do with this. I don't even know why you're talking to me."

His eyes suddenly narrowed. "In fact, I don't like what you're implying. Roosevelt was the better team on Saturday. That's all there is to it."

Abruptly, Todd turned back to his engine, signaling that this interview was over. I looked at Ollie. He shrugged. I wasn't sure how to read Todd's comments. We were almost out of the garage when Todd called us back.

"Don't tell me *Marsh* is behind this?" Todd said, chuckling. "I never realized what a sore loser he is. Central had a great season. And now Marsh is just cheapening it by acting like this. Well, you tell him . . . " Todd paused. "Forget it, I'll tell him myself."

And that was that. As Ollie and I pedaled home, I tried to figure out what to make of Todd Donlin. He was a man who clearly hated Coach Marsh. However, nothing in what he had said indicated he had it in for the Vikings. Todd remained one big question mark.

Δ   Δ   Δ

Nina was not waiting for us when we returned to my office. And because I wanted to get this new information into my computer while it was still fresh in my mind, Ollie decided to go check out T.J. Hardy himself. We weren't sure if Nina had had time to talk to him.

We had nothing but hunches to go on at this point, but I still believed that someone had given a Viking playbook to Roosevelt. There really is something to be said for detective's intuition. It has helped me in more than a few cases in the past.

Anyway, I knew that we would have to prove something soon if we wanted the County Football Commission to declare last week's game a forfeit. That *was* the point, after all. If the commission found Roosevelt guilty of cheating, Central would have a shot at the county championship. But the championship game was just a few days away, and if we didn't get some concrete evidence soon, we would never convince the football commission in time.

After putting Todd's interview into my computer, I stared at the screen for about 10 minutes. Then I flipped the computer off and headed outside to my office.

"Hey, Jack!" Nina called out as she walked up my driveway. "How'd it go?" I asked her, putting the basketball down on the driveway and sitting on it, waiting to hear what she had discovered.

"Well, it was interesting . . . " Nina began, and then paused. She loves to keep me in suspense. But she's a great associate and a terrific friend, so I put up with these little quirks. I didn't say anything. I just waited patiently for her to get to the point. Once she saw that she was not going to be able to bait me, Nina continued. "I went to see T.J. Hardy first. What a creep!"

"Really?" I asked. So far, no one had been all that difficult. I was surprised that T.J. would be. I don't know why I thought that since I didn't even know him.

"He practically slammed the door in my face when I told him about our theory," Nina continued, frowning.

Now, that *was* interesting, I thought.

"Then I went over to Marty Frank's," Nina said. "Now, *he* was very cooperative. But you could tell that he and T.J.

just do not get along. Marty is sure that Central lost because T.J. played with so little intensity. He told me that T.J. is usually very aggressive on the field and will even chew people out if they blow plays or if they don't seem into the game." Nina paused to take a breath. "I think that T.J. Hardy had something to do with it. I did not like him one single bit, Jack."

"You didn't like T.J.?" Ollie exclaimed in surprise, suddenly walking up behind us.

I turned to look at him. "You *did*?" I asked.

"Great guy," Ollie answered, frowning at Nina. "Are you sure that you didn't say anything to make him mad? I hear he loses his temper kind of fast, but I think he's pretty cool."

"I just told him what we think caused the Vikings to lose on Saturday," Nina explained, shaking her head. "Then I asked him if I could talk to him for a few minutes. And as I told Jack, he practically slammed the door in my face."

"That's really bizarre," Ollie commented, confused. "I said exactly the same thing you did about our theory, and he invited me in. He had been working out in his garage and was just about to drink a protein shake or something. Major muscles on that guy."

Ollie sometimes gets off the track—especially about anything concerning sports.

"Anyway, T.J. seemed kind of upset about the game," Ollie continued. "He told me that he was trying to win a scholarship to a Big Ten school. In fact, he's already had a couple of offers."

"Really?" I asked. "Even though the Vikings lost the game?"

"Sure," Ollie answered. "That game doesn't really say much about the rest of the season."

Nina didn't say anything. T.J. Hardy must have been really rude to her if she was at a loss for words.

"Still, I don't think he was very good *last* year," I said, trying to dredge up an image of last year's team. "In fact, I don't know if he even started."

"Oh, yeah," Ollie said suddenly. "I forgot to tell you that as I was leaving T.J.'s, Milo came walking up to the door."

"Milo?" Nina exclaimed. "I hope you didn't tell him why you were there."

"Are you kidding?" Ollie exclaimed indignantly. "He would be all over us if he knew about our theory. He can be like a leech when he's onto a story."

While Milo sometimes gets in the way of our investigations, I know it's because he has an ace reporter's nose for news. I said as much to my associates. "And, he really does do some good," I continued, trying to convince them—and myself, too. "Don't you remember that series of articles he wrote last month about steroid use?"

"Oh, yeah," Ollie conceded. "That was a good series."

"Really," Nina agreed. "I never realized that so many kids use steroids. I mean, at least six percent of all high school seniors—that's an awful lot!"

"Awful is right," I said. "Steroids are so dangerous—they're drugs, and they can cause liver damage, acne, hostility, violent mood swings and an increase in risk factors for heart disease." I paused. We were really getting off the track now. "Anyway, Milo isn't that bad. He's just annoying sometimes."

"Speaking of drugs," Ollie began, "Wells told me that he had heard some rumor that the County Athletic Commission was going to start a mandatory drug testing program on championship level high school athletics—beginning with the upcoming county football championship game."

"Really?" Nina asked. Ollie nodded. "Well, it's about time."

I had to get my crew back on track. "Guys, I think it's time to talk to Coach Devitt," I said, waiting for their reactions.

"Do you think he'll talk to us?" Ollie asked. "I mean, I hear he's not the most personable of guys."

"He'd better," I said. "He's our best lead so far. If the Tigers had seen a Viking playbook, Devitt would know about it. Let's go see what we can find out."

We hopped on our bikes and headed over to Roosevelt High School.

Δ   Δ   Δ

The football team was just leaving the field for the locker room as we screeched to a stop near the bleachers. Coach Devitt was sitting there writing something on a clipboard. We walked over to him.

Gus Devitt is a short, stocky, square-jawed man who looks to be in his early fifties. And he always seems to be scowling. I really hoped he would talk to us.

"Coach Devitt?" I asked, as we approached him. He looked up, scowling. I pushed my glasses up on my nose and plunged on. "My name is Jack B. Quick, and these are my associates, Ollie Steele and Nina Chin."

"Quick? Aren't you that kid detective?" Coach Devitt asked, tapping his pencil against the top of his clipboard. "What do you want with me?"

"Well . . . " I began. But, of course, Nina could not let me finish.

"We just have a couple of questions to ask you, if you don't mind," Nina said. At least she hadn't told him we thought his team had a copy of the Viking playbook. He would probably boot us off the field in a flat minute if he knew that.

"What questions?" the coach asked impatiently.

"What amazed me about the game," Ollie cut in, "was the way your guys seemed to know what Central was going to do even before they did it. You must have done some serious scouting before that game."

The coach did not seem to realize that Ollie had not really asked him a question—he had just made an observation. Luckily, Coach Devitt replied.

"I guess it seemed that way," the coach said, laughing. "But the Vikings play like a bunch of robots, always running the same plays. They're easy to follow. Besides, Roosevelt's got the superior coach," he concluded with a smug half-smile.

I had to bite my tongue. The Vikings happen to have some of the most innovative plays on the high school level.

27

"Your defense played almost if they had E.S.P. or something," Ollie continued, shooting a quick glance at me. "Even your offense seemed to know when the Viking defense was going to blitz."

This time the coach noticed that Ollie was not really asking questions, but merely voicing opinions. "Just what is it that you're asking me?" he barked.

"Is this your first league title?" Nina asked quickly. It was a good thing one of us was trying to get some concrete information. And her well-timed question stopped the coach short.

"We should have won a few others," he grumbled. "But I wasn't going to let this one slip through my fingers. I covered all the bases to make sure we would win. All my boys had to do was execute the plays. And they did."

Coach Devitt suddenly slammed his pencil against his clipboard, breaking the point. "Look, if that's all you have to ask me, I really have got to prepare for this weekend's game," he said, irritated. "In case you've forgotten, *Roosevelt* has to play in the county championship." With that, he stood and stomped off to the locker room, leaving the three of us standing there.

We just looked at each other, our mouths hanging open in shock at his outburst. Then we slowly got up and headed back to our bikes. Coach Devitt certainly had a forceful personality.

Δ   Δ   Δ

I stopped by Coach Marsh's office the next day after school to fill him in on what we had learned so far. And I had to admit that it wasn't very much to go on.

"Well, keep it up, Jack," the coach said after I had finished my update. "It's too bad we don't have some sort of proof that a playbook was copied. At least then we could go to the County Athletic Commission and get them to put a hold on this weekend's game while you solved the case."

I nodded. I didn't really think the commission would believe detective's intuition at this point. But we were getting close; I could feel it.

"I've got all the playbooks right here," Coach Marsh continued, jerking his head toward the huge pile of loose-leaf binders stacked on the windowsill. "You know, Jack," he went on, and then paused. He ran a hand through his thinning hair. "I've been thinking. What if the Tigers just had a good day? Besides that, Joe Tabor plays on their team now. He could have told them some of our plays and formations."

"Who's Joe Tabor?" I asked, curious because I hadn't heard that name before.

"He played for me last year, but his family moved in July," the coach replied. "He plays a pretty good right tackle."

I found that fact rather interesting. We needed to talk to Joe Tabor.

After I finished with Coach Marsh, I went out to round up Ollie and Nina. Unfortunately, Ollie was nowhere to be found. So Nina and I headed back over to Roosevelt.

The football team was running laps when we got there. Nina and I hung back for a while, watching the practice. We did not want Coach Devitt to see us hanging around his field. If he spotted us, he would probably have a cow.

Nina and I had someone point out Joe Tabor for us and we caught up with him after practice when he came out of the locker room, showered and changed.

"Joe Tabor, could we talk to you for a minute?" I called out, as we jogged up to him.

He turned around and stopped, waiting for us. "Who are you?"

"I'm Jack B. Quick, sports detective, and this is Nina Chin," I said, introducing us.

Joe held out his hand and I shook it. "What can I do for you?" he asked, grinning.

"Well, Joe, we're investigating last week's game against Central," Nina said. "We were wondering how the Vikings could get blown out like that."

Joe laughed. "Hey, you should know that, Jack," he said to me. "Sports are a tricky thing to predict. It's the world of the unexpected. We just played a great game."

"Of course, it probably helped that you played for Coach Marsh last year," Nina went on.

"I guess you're pretty familiar with the Viking signals and plays and stuff like that," I put in.

"Yeah, I guess that helped a little," Joe agreed. "I mean Marsh only has so many plays, so I know most of them—the Double Pump, the Boomerang. He's got to come up with something new. That's probably why we beat his team. Coach Devitt is much more creative."

Nina and I nodded, but I disagreed. I know for a fact

that Marsh is creative. We thanked Joe for his time. Nina had a piano lesson, so I headed back to Marsh's office alone. I was feeling pretty depressed.

The coach was just where I had left him, sitting behind his desk. He looked up as soon as I walked in and sat down.

"You know, Coach Marsh," I began slowly, "I think you might have been right. Joe Tabor seems pretty familiar with all of your plays. I think he may have just passed that information along to Coach Devitt. There's nothing illegal in that."

Coach Marsh sighed heavily. "I was afraid of that," he said softly. "Thank you for all your help, Jack."

"I just wish it could have turned out differently," I said, slouching down farther in my seat. Something was still nagging at me, though. Something did not feel right. My detective's intuition kept telling me that this case was not yet closed.

"Me, too," the coach agreed. "My boys worked so hard this season. They really deserved to win that title. You know, they even learned twelve new plays for the game on Saturday. I guess I'll just have to save them for next season, especially the Boomerang."

Suddenly, I sat up straight. It was good to know that my intuition was not failing me. "Did you say Boomerang?" I asked excitedly.

Startled, the coach managed a "Yes. Why?" before I cut him off.

"Coach, Joe Tabor told me that he knew all of your old plays," I said. "He even went so far as to say that maybe if you had developed some new plays and been a little more creative, Central might have had a chance. And . . . " I paused dramatically, "he mentioned the Boomerang play by name. Are you sure that you didn't use that play last year?"

The coach started looking interested. "Positive," he said firmly. "I went to this big conference over the summer and one of the directors helped me work up that play. I wanted to save it for something major. And I did."

"But it looks as if someone else knew that play as well," I pointed out. "Coach, do you think I could look through those playbooks?" I didn't know what they were going to tell me, but it was worth a shot. I knew then that I had been right all along: Roosevelt had had a copy of the Viking playbook before the game. Coach Marsh gave me the go-ahead to look at the playbooks and excused himself to attend a short faculty meeting. He asked me to lock up if I finished before he returned.

I sat down and started going through the books. They all looked the same, but I felt as if I had to go through each one anyway. Otherwise, I would not feel as if I had covered all the bases.

Finally, near the bottom of the stack, I uncovered something interesting—*very* interesting. I closed the playbook in question to look at the cover. The name on it surprised me somewhat. It was someone whom I had never strongly suspected. Now all I needed was a motive.

I scribbled the coach a note telling him what I had discovered and asking him to gather certain people in his office the next day after school. Then I turned off the lights and locked the door behind me. I had to get home and call Ollie and Nina to bring them both up to date.

Δ   Δ   Δ

The next afternoon, we gathered in Coach Marsh's office. The coach was there with Mr. Jacobs from the County Athletic Commission and, of course, Nina, Ollie and myself. We were waiting for two more people.

We stood around uncomfortably, not saying much. Mr. Jacobs looked sternly at all of us. Coach Marsh had told me during lunch period that the athletic commissioners had taken a dim view of my accusations. It was their feeling that Coach Marsh just did not know when to concede. They felt Central had lost, fair and square. It was up to me to prove otherwise.

Finally, the door opened and Joe Tabor stepped in. "Hi, Coach," he said, hesitantly. "What's up?" He looked around at Mr. Jacobs, and then he noticed us. He scowled and sat down. He must have known that the gig was up.

A few minutes later, someone else knocked and stepped into the room: T.J. Hardy. Big and hulking, T.J. took up a lot of space. He looked around and when his eyes lit on Joe Tabor he sat down and looked at the floor.

I cleared my throat. "Hello, everybody," I began. "I'm glad you could all make it."

Mr. Jacobs frowned at me, so I got right to the point.

"After the game last Saturday, I had a feeling that things were not as they seemed. Central had been beaten too soundly," I began. Mr. Jacobs harrumphed. "Now, I know that anything can happen in the course of a football game,

33

but what happened was a little too weird to be a matter of chance," I continued. "The Tigers seemed to anticipate plays by reading the Vikings' formations and signals before the ball was snapped. That led me to the conclusion that perhaps the Tigers had an unfair advantage.

"After tracking down a number of suspects, Joe Tabor provided me with my first real clue. He said that Coach Marsh had to get some new plays going, instead of just running the same old ones. Joe played for Central last year, and is on Roosevelt this year," I explained to Mr. Jacobs. "Anyway, he mentioned the Boomerang as one of Central's tired plays. Coach Marsh told me yesterday that until two weeks ago, even his own players did not know about the Boomerang, a play that he had just invented this past summer. How then, could Joe have known about it?" I paused and took a breath.

"This proved that the Tigers did indeed have a copy of Central's playbook. The question was how did they get it?" I asked. Rhetorical questions are always a good device to keep a tough audience's attention. "Well, I went through all the playbooks last night, and I found that one was different from the rest. Yours," I said, pointing at T.J. "Some of the pages had two tag numbers running along the right-hand side. Now, we all know that those tags are attached to every school's copy machine. Central's tag is 645. I checked it at lunch today. I also called the Roosevelt office today. Their's is 8765. T.J.'s book had both numbers on the edge."

Everyone just started at me silently. "T.J., you gave a copy of your book to Joe, didn't you?" I asked. T.J. nodded slowly. He had been caught with the goods, so to speak, and it would not have done him any good to deny it. "And Joe accidentally mixed some of his copies in with the original.

"My next problem was motive," I continued, confidently. Unveiling the motive is my favorite part of a case. "Why in the world would you want to ruin an undefeated season in your senior year? Ollie gave me the piece to that puzzle. You heard a rumor that there would be drug testing at the county championship game this year. I looked up your stats in last year's program. You really put on a lot of weight in the off season, didn't you?"

T.J. just stared at his sneakers, not even looking at me.

"Then I remembered how you were so nasty when Nina came to see you yet so nice when Ollie dropped by less than a half hour later. And then there's your acne," I said.

Mr. Jacobs looked at me blankly. I think he had been following me up until this point.

"T.J., are you on steriods?" Coach Marsh asked suddenly.

"I only did it because I wanted to be the best I could be," T.J. blurted out. "I really wanted that scholarship. When I visited the university over the summer, a couple of the linemen said I needed another 50 to 60 pounds to play Big Ten ball and that steroids would make me bigger and stronger in a hurry. They told me everybody used them."

"So why did you throw the game?" Mr. Jacobs asked.

"The drug test," T.J. answered immediately.

Nina, Ollie and I got up to go. We had done our part. It was up to Commissioner Jacobs and the coaches to tie up the loose ends of *The Case of the "Missing" Playbook.*

Δ   Δ   Δ

Three days later, I was playing hoops with Ollie in my driveway. He was, of course, beating me 17-11. But at least I was close.

"So, Coach Devitt was suspended pending further investigation?" Ollie asked.

"That's right," I said, panting. "They figured that the coach knew about the playbook. In fact, they think he copied Joe's copy and passed it out to all of his players."

Ollie stopped for a second with the ball tucked under his arm and resting on his hip. "It's too bad about T.J., though," he said.

"I know," I replied, taking the opportunity to breathe. "He was pressured into doing something really dangerous— and illegal."

"What's going to happen to him?" Ollie asked, dribbling the ball behind his back.

"I don't know," I replied. "I'm sure he'll lose his scholarship. But who knows, maybe he'll turn up at some small college, playing without steroids, and tear up the conference."

"I certainly hope so," Ollie said, getting set to play again. "He's really not a bad guy."

"No, but steroids can do such terrible things to your body that they can make you *seem* like a bad guy," I replied. "He's lucky he got caught so soon—those drugs could have really messed up his life for good."

And with that, Ollie drove around me to sink another

shot in the basket. I was really going to have to work on my inside defense.

Case closed.

 # The Case of the Wiped-out Windsurfer

"Go for it, Nina!" I shouted from the sideline. One of Nina Chin's teammates in the front row had set the volleyball high and close to the net. Nina crouched down and sprang up to spike it over the net. The other team's forward dove for it, but ended up sprawled in the sand. Game point!

Nina's team started to cheer. As I moved forward to congratulate her, someone tapped me on the shoulder. I turned around.

"Jack B. Quick?" the guy asked.

I pushed my glasses up my nose and gave him a once-over. He was about 18 years old, with reddish-blond hair and pale blue eyes in a tanned, freckled face. His feet were bare, and he wore loud flower-patterned jams and a royal blue wetsuit top, unzipped. "That's me," I replied.

"You're the dude who's the sports detective?" he asked.

"Right again," I answered. I decided to throw in a free

sample of my detective work to prove it. "Is boardsailing as much fun as they say? I've been thinking about giving it a try."

The guy's blue eyes widened in surprise. "You know who I am?"

"Nope, just what you do," I told him, smiling. "You're wearing a wetsuit, which could mean you're into scuba diving, but nobody wears jams diving. You could be a surfer, but when I noticed the calluses on your hands from hanging onto a boom, I figured you had to be a windsurfer."

"Cool," he said. "You really are a detective."

I'd done enough showing off, so I just said, "Can I help you?"

"I hope so," he replied in a gloomy voice, knitting his eyebrows and frowning. "Something weird is going on around here, and I can't decide if somebody is trying to wreck the whole Sail-Off or if some dude's out to get *me* in particular. You know what the Sail-Off is, right?"

"Sure," I said. Who didn't? There were flyers on all the bulletin boards and telephone poles near the beach. Freddie Ho's Surf Shop was sponsoring a full weekend of windsurfing contests. The person with the highest point total would win a round-trip ticket to the upcoming World Championships in Hawaii.

"Oh, you found him. Good," said my associate, Ollie Steele, as he joined us. He had a sketch pad under his arm, so I figured he wanted to draw some windsurfing scenes. Ollie loves to capture action scenes on paper. "I told Dave to talk to you about his problem, Jack," Ollie added.

"Dave?" I questioned, raising one eyebrow.

"My name's Dave Marsh," the windsurfer replied.

"Dave's a top-flight windsurfer," Ollie told me. "One of the best anywhere around here. He's the favorite to win that trip to Hawaii."

"You mean I *was* the favorite," Dave corrected sourly. "Not any more. My old red van got two flats on the way here, which made me miss the first heat of the freestyle competition. That's the part where we get to do all the tricks and jumps over the waves."

"That could have been an accident," I suggested.

"Uh huh, sure," Dave replied, sarcastically. "But how about this? When I finally got here, I started rigging up for the speed trials, in which we make two runs from point-to-point, just for speed. But I couldn't get the drawstring untied on my sail bag. I finally had to cut it. It turned out that there was glue on the slide fastener." Dave shrugged, and I could hear the frustration in his voice. "That's usually my best event, but by the time I got rigged, I was so flustered that I couldn't pull better than third place."

Ollie asked, "Is there any way you could have spilled glue on the fastener without noticing? Maybe when you were busy using it for something else?"

Dave gave Ollie an impatient look and shook his head. "The stuff on my bag is clear," he said. "I only use white glue. Besides, I think I'd remember if I'd spilled it on my sail bag."

"Hold on for a second," I said. "I think Nina should hear this." I looked around and saw that Nina was still talking to some of the other volleyball players. I caught her eye and beckoned for her to join us when she could.

A moment later, Nina walked up to us, carrying her gym bag and wiping her forehead with the towel around her neck. "Hi, guys. What's up?" she asked.

"Dave, this is my other associate, Nina Chin," I said. I quickly filled Nina in on what might be our next case.

"Hmm," Nina murmured thoughtfully. "Have any of the other windsurfers been having problems?" she asked.

"Well . . . no one else has said anything, and I think I would have heard about it," Dave replied.

"Then, if somebody really is doing these things on purpose, it looks like you're the target," I said, confidently. "Is there anyone you can think of who might be out to get you? Do you have any enemies?"

"Enemies?" Dave hesitated, then said, "No way."

"How about rivals?" Ollie questioned. "Somebody who would do anything to win the Sail-Off this weekend?"

Instead of answering, Dave turned away and looked out across the water. He seemed to be staring at a little clump of multicolored sails. I tried to follow his line of sight, but it was hopeless. He could have been looking at any one of half a dozen sailboards, or he could have been watching a seagull skim over the waves.

Ollie pressed his point. "You've won a lot of events, Dave. Who usually comes in second?"

"That's ridiculous," Dave replied. "Jason would never—I mean—"

"Jason Willard?" Ollie asked quickly. Obviously, he'd

been keeping tabs on the local windsurfing scene. "He's a tall guy with brown hair and a limp, isn't he?"

Dave nodded reluctantly. "That's the dude. He broke his leg badly when he was a kid and it healed wrong. When you think of it, it's pretty awesome that he's turned himself into such a great windsurfer."

"Good enough to beat you in a fair meet?" I asked, watching Dave's eyes carefully. He looked off to the right, away from my gaze.

"Well . . . if I'm having a bad day and he's having a good one, sure," Dave mumbled. "Listen, do you think you can help me, or not? I really—"

He broke off suddenly, and his face turned pale. I looked over to the right. Two people were passing by, about 20 feet away. One of them I recognized as Freddie Ho, the sponsor of the Sail-Off. The guy next to him, leaning over to talk to him, was tall, with brown hair and he walked with a limp. Behind them, out over the water, a small, open plane called an ultra-light buzzed past, looking like a huge dragonfly.

"Is that Jason Willard?" I asked Dave.

"What?" Dave looked in my direction, his eyes glazed and unfocused. Then he blinked and said, "Oh. Yeah. That's him. But I'm telling you, he wouldn't pull anything that low. I've known him for a long time, and he's just not that kind of dude."

"Somebody is," said Nina. "And if we don't find our culprit pretty soon, you can probably forget about winning that trip to the Hawaiian Islands."

"Nina's right," I agreed. "We'd better get to work."

"Great. I'll catch you later," Dave replied.

As he walked off, I turned to Ollie and Nina. "I hope I'm wrong, but this is starting to look like *The Case of the Wiped-Out Windsurfer*. Come on, let's question this dude Jason." I could really get into this windsurfer lingo.

We caught up to Dave's rival near the judges' stand. He was using a pair of binoculars to watch the windsurfers on the lake, which gave me a moment to check him out. I asked Nina to give me my binoculars, which were in her gym bag. Jason, who appeared to be around 19 or 20, was wearing a black and fluorescent yellow wetsuit top, matching shorts and a Portland Trailblazers hat. I liked him on sight.

"Jason Willard?" I called. He turned around, smiling.

"Yeah, I'm Jason. How ya doin'?" he asked.

I introduced myself and my associates, then added, "Dave Marsh asked us to find out if somebody's trying to sabotage the Sail-Off. A couple of weird things have happened to him, and they don't seem to be accidents."

"Oh, yeah?" Jason said. "Listen, dude, he didn't accuse me, did he? Because there is no way—"

Ollie broke in. "Hey, man! It's not like that. Dave said you really know what's what and could help us."

"Oh," Jason replied. He glanced around, then asked, "What kind of help?"

I adjusted my glasses. "First of all, have you had any problems with your equipment today—suspicious accidents, dirty tricks, sabotage?" I asked. "Or have you heard of anyone else who has?"

Jason shook his head. "Nope. Windsurfing puts a lot of strain on your equipment, though, you know. Things break sometimes when you don't expect it—usually at the worst possible time. But sabotage? Not that I know of."

"Would you say Dave Marsh is the favorite to win the trip to Hawaii?" asked Ollie.

"I'm insulted by that question," Jason said with a grin. "I'll have you know my bag's already packed! But really, if you'd asked me that two or three weeks ago, the answer would have been obvious. Dave was definitely the dude to beat. Not now. Dave's been off his form—*way* off. With the mistakes he's been making, he'll be lucky to stay in the top five. Win? No way."

"Have you known Dave a long time?" I inquired.

"We go back a ways. Why?" Jason asked curiously.

"Has he had slumps like this before?" I continued. "Or do you think these dirty tricks are getting on his nerves?"

Jason shrugged and pushed his hair back behind his ear. "We all have our ups and downs," he said. "Like the time a bunch of us decided to go to California for a big competition. We were all nervous, and we all went into a slump. But Dave was the worst. And I mean *worst*!"

"What happened to him?" Nina asked.

"He was so nervous before we left that he kept falling off his board," Jason told us. "And he got so worried about trusting his board to the airline baggage handlers that he finally decided to take the train instead. He had to leave a couple of days before the rest of us because the train only makes that trip twice a week. Once we were at the event, we all settled down to business. I remember Dave racked up some very nice times."

"That's a long trip by train," Ollie put in.

"Yeah, about twelve hours. I thought about doing it with him, but I didn't want to spend the money on two extra nights in a hotel room."

"Jason," I began slowly, "if Dave isn't at his best, for whatever reason, that makes you the favorite to win that trip to Hawaii, doesn't it?"

Under his dark tan, Jason's face turned red. "I've got a good shot at it, sure," he said in a level tone. "But I always did. I don't need dirty tricks to win—just a good wind and a little luck." His voice rose. "And I'd like to have a little talk with anyone who says different!"

"Chill out," Ollie said with a smile. "Jack wasn't accusing you of anything."

"Of course not," I cut in quickly. "My next question was going to be, can you think of anyone who might want to spoil the Sail-Off?"

"Spoil the Sail-Off?" Jason shook his head. "No way. This is an awesome event for all the windsurfers around here. It's a chance to get together and see what we can do against each other. It's great publicity for the sport, too. You've got to admire Freddie for coming up with the idea and following through on it, in spite of everything."

Nina jumped in. "In spite of what? Were there some problems?"

Jason shrugged his shoulders. "A few buttoned-up sailboat types were against the Sail-Off, that's all. I guess they think this is their beach, or something. But the rumor is—" He fell silent and glanced around again.

"Is what?" I prompted, stepping a little closer.

Jason frowned. "Just that, from what I hear, Freddie's Surf Shop hasn't been doing as well as he hoped. Some of the guys are saying that if he can't turn it around fast, he'll have to close down. So I guess you could say he's betting the business on this meet. If the Sail-Off goes down the tube, so does his shop." Then he added, "Listen, guys, I've got to run. I'm in the next event."

"Good luck," I said.

"Yeah, thanks, same to you dudes." Jason turned and hurried away as fast as he could.

"Hmm," I said. "Did either of you get the feeling that he suddenly wanted to get away from us?"

"I thought he seemed pretty nervous from the start," Nina commented. "What about you, Ollie?"

Ollie was staring after Jason. "What?" he asked, looking at Nina. "Oh, yeah. I guess so. But did you guys notice what Jason had in the back pocket of his shorts?" He stopped and gave us a significant look.

"Well?" Nina asked eagerly. "What was it?"

"A small white tube with a red cap," Ollie replied. "And I don't think it was toothpaste. It looked like model airplane cement to me."

"In other words, glue," I said. "If you're right, the next question is, what kind of glue was used on Dave's sail bag? Let's go find him and take a look."

"Too late," said Nina. "There he goes."

She pointed over my shoulder. I looked around, holding up my binoculars. A board with a rainbow-striped sail was heading out toward open water. It was too far away to see the rider's face, but he was wearing flowered jams and a blue wetsuit top.

"Rats!" I said. "It must be time for one of the events he's competing in."

As if the announcer had heard me, a loudspeaker crackled to life. "O.K., everybody," the voice said. "We're about to start the next round of speed trials. Our contestants each make two runs, one from north to south, the other from south to north. Whoever has the lowest average time on both runs combined, wins."

"Let's move closer to the judges' stand," I suggested. "We'll get a better view from there."

A bunch of other spectators apparently had the same idea. The crowd near the judges' stand was so thick that I led Ollie and Nina up onto the grass behind the beach, where we could see what was happening out on the lake.

Off to our left, eight or ten sailboards were moving around in big circles, waiting for their turns. One of them peeled off and began to sail parallel to the beach, about 30 yards offshore. I put down the binoculars to get the big picture.

"Here we go," Ollie called. "There's the first contestant. I wonder when it's Dave's turn."

The sailboard picked up speed as it entered the trial zone. I watched for a moment. Then I noticed Freddie Ho and a dark-haired man wearing expensive sunglasses walk-

47

ing toward us. Whatever they were talking about seemed to interest them a lot more than the speed trials.

The two men stopped about 10 feet away and stood, side by side, facing the ocean. Neither of them noticed me as I slowly edged toward them.

"Freddie," the dark-haired man was saying, "it's you I'm thinking about. You're this far from having to close your doors, and once that happens, your name and goodwill are worth exactly *zip*. I'm making you a fair offer, but it won't last forever."

Freddie looked tense, but his voice stayed calm. "My shop's in good shape, Donald," he said. "The publicity from the Sail-Off has brought in a lot of business. The truth is that I'd be doing even better if you'd stop undercutting me every step of the way."

The man in the sunglasses turned his head, giving Freddie a smile that reminded me of a shark. "That's just honest competition," he protested. "Lower prices are good for the customer."

"Oh, sure. And what'll happen to the prices at your shop if I'm out of the picture?" Freddie asked. "They'll go sky-high!"

Freddie paused, then said, "Listen, Donald. I was one of the first windsurfers around here. My original shop was in my garage. I've done more than anybody to build the sport and make it popular. I've got a responsibility to the people I've brought into it, and I'm not selling them out to a big chain like yours."

Donald Sturdevant said, "I respect that, my friend, but

you may not have a choice. I know the kind of bind you're in. What happens if you can't find the cash to pay for that round-trip ticket to Hawaii? How do you think your wind-surfer friends will feel about that?"

Freddie clenched his fists. "That's not going to happen," he growled. "I've got plenty—" Then he noticed me standing there and broke off.

I stared past them toward the water, pretending to be absorbed in the speed trials. No good. A moment later the two men walked away. But they left me with more than a lot to think about.

"Hey, Jack!" Ollie exclaimed. "That was some run Dave made, wasn't it?"

"Was it?" I questioned, rejoining Ollie and Nina where they were standing on the grass.

"Where have *you* been?" Nina asked, laughing.

"Collecting a new suspect," I announced, pushing my glasses up my nose. "No, I take that back—*two* new suspects." I quickly filled my associates in on what I had overheard.

Ollie whistled. "Sturdevant's Sports is a major-league chain," he told me. "They've got stores all over Oregon. Do you think he's sabotaging the meet to force Freddie Ho to sell the Surf Shop?"

"He sounded awfully eager to get Freddie to sell," I said, cautiously. "And I get the feeling he's not the kind of guy who'd worry about doing something underhanded. Not if that's what it takes to get what he wants."

Nina nodded slowly. "And you think he's working with

49

someone else," she stated. "That makes sense. A guy like that probably doesn't do his own dirty work. Who do you think his accomplice is?"

I gave Nina a puzzled look. "I didn't say anything about an accomplice."

"Sure you did," she replied. "You said you had two new suspects."

"Let me put it this way," I said. "What happens if those dirty tricks aren't stopped?"

"I guess they'd have to call off the event," Ollie answered. "Or at least throw out the results. If some performances have been affected by tricks, how can you tell who the real winner should be?"

"Then who gets the trip to Hawaii?" I continued.

Ollie shrugged. "No one, I guess." His eyes opened wide. "Wait a minute. . . . You don't think Freddie Ho would wreck his own contest on purpose just to get out of buying that ticket, do you?"

"I'm not saying he *would*," I said. "But from what we know, it could be a good motive. If he waited till near the end to call off the competition, he would get just as much publicity as if the event had finished. Maybe even more since it would make a great story. And then he wouldn't have to fork over the money for the plane ticket—money he may not even have."

"It makes sense as a motive," Nina agreed, nodding. "But so does Sturdevant's, not to mention Jason's. How do we figure out which one is responsible?"

"We investigate," I exclaimed, making a sweeping

gesture with my right arm. "Boldly. But let's not forget another possibility."

"Which is?" asked Ollie.

"Maybe *none* of our suspects is responsible," I replied. "After all, what are we investigating? Two flat tires and glue spilled on the slide fastener of Dave's sail bag. And we only have his word for it that he didn't spill the glue himself."

"Oh, come on," Ollie began heatedly, "you're not going to tell us—"

"It seems pretty clear that no one else has been hit by dirty tricks, doesn't it?" I pointed out. "What if Dave's just spooked and *imagines* that someone is out to get him? Don't forget that story Jason told us about Dave taking the train to a contest because he didn't want to trust his sailboard to the airlines. That sounds like the kind of guy who gets nervous pretty easily."

"Well, if you're right," Nina said, "then we can relax. The case is solved. There won't be any more dirty tricks because there never were any."

"Look," said Ollie, pointing toward the water. "Dave's getting set for his second run. If he can do as well as he did in the other direction, he's got the event cinched."

Picking up my binoculars again, I watched the rainbow-striped sail come around and begin to pick up speed. Dave was holding onto the wishbone, which runs along the bottom of the sail, and leaning way back, practically sitting on the water. He was trying to keep his board flat and still get as much power from the sail as he could. Spray hissed up over the front of his board as it sliced through the water.

"Awesome!" Ollie shouted. "Look at that! He's got it in the bag."

Dave was nearly in front of the judges' stand now. He shifted his rear foot a few inches, then moved his right hand farther back on the wishbone, to coax a little more speed out of his board. An instant later, he was doing a back somersault into the water.

The spectators gasped as the sail came down on top of Dave. The lifeguard boat sped over to help him, but then Dave's head appeared bobbing in the water next to his board. He grabbed the end of his mast and started towing his board to the beach.

"Come on," I urged Nina and Ollie. "I didn't like the looks of that fall."

We ran down the slope to the water's edge, getting there just in time to help Dave drag his sailboard up onto the sand.

"What happened, Dave?" Ollie asked. "Are you O.K.?"

"I'm fine," Dave said, shortly. "I just wiped out."

"We saw that part," I said, nodding. "But why?"

Dave looked up at me from where he was kneeling next to the sail. "Come here, dudes," he said. He lifted the sail by the rear edge and pointed to the back section of the wishbone. "Feel that."

I stooped down and ran my hand over the metal tube. There was a lot of sand stuck to it, but under the sand I could feel something slippery. Something like grease.

I looked up at Dave. "You don't usually grease this thing, do you?" I asked.

He snorted. "Give me a break!" he exclaimed. "The

whole point is to have as good a grip as possible. Somebody didn't want me to."

I sniffed my fingers and wrinkled my nose. "It smells like coconut oil," I said. "My bet is that somebody smeared suntan lotion on your wishbone. But why didn't you spot it before?"

"You don't windsurf, do you?" Dave replied. "When I'm just tooling around, my grip is usually near the center of the wishbone. The only time I'm likely to go for a grip that far back is when I'm really cooking on a close reach. That's when the front of the board is pointed as close as possible to the direction the wind is coming from. To catch the wind, you have to pull the sail in to the center of the board. On the first run, there were two differences: I was closer to the front of the board, and I was on the other side of the sail."

I wrinkled my brow and thought hard. "Since the two runs were in opposite directions, does that mean you were definitely going to be on one side of the sail one time and the other the next time?"

"Unless the wind shifted a lot, sure," Dave said. "Why?"

"Don't you see? Whoever put that gunk there has to know something about windsurfing," I answered. "They knew that you weren't likely to discover it before the speed trials, and that it was practically sure to throw you during one of your two runs."

"Good thinking, Jack!" Ollie exclaimed.

I felt myself blushing. "Thanks," I said. A sound like a lawn mower caught my attention. I glanced up. The ultra-light plane was just coming into view again over the treetops. As it passed close overhead, the pilot, completely exposed on his little seat, waved to the crowd on the beach. He was near enough for me to make out the red and gold stripe on his helmet.

I waited until the tiny plane flew out over the water, then said, "Now, where does this take us? All three of our main suspects know something about windsurfing, but Jason and Freddie are experts, and Sturdevant is not."

"Jason? Freddie?" Dave stammered. "No way, dude! It can't be!" I glanced at him. His face had paled, making his freckles stand out and tiny droplets of sweat were gathering along his hairline.

"Hey, are you O.K.?" I questioned him. "You look awful."

"I'm fine," Dave said, wiping his hand across his forehead. "I just can't believe that Jason or Freddie would pull something like this. In fact, I'm positive they wouldn't. Those dudes are friends of mine. Maybe you should lay off hassling them."

"You're the one who asked us to investigate," Ollie pointed out. "It's not our fault if you don't exactly like what we find out."

"I know," Dave said. "But I think I made a mistake. I had no business asking you to spy on my friends. Anyway, the more I think about it, the more it looks as if I've just been having some bad luck."

"What about the glue on your sail bag?" asked Nina.

"And the slippery stuff on your wishbone?" Ollie

54

added. "That 'bad luck' kept you from winning the speed trial. Are you saying it got there by accident?"

Dave's face began to turn red. "Look," he said in a strained voice. "I know you dudes are only trying to help. I appreciate that. But what I'd appreciate a whole lot more is for you to let it ride. O.K.? You catch my drift? Just drop it!"

I glanced at Nina and Ollie. "Sure, Dave. We understand," I said. "Come on, guys, let's go find a good spot to watch the rest of the Sail-Off."

"But, Jack—" Ollie began. I looked at him and gave him just the merest shake of my head. "Never mind," he said. "See ya, Dave. Good luck."

As soon as we were out of earshot, Ollie grabbed my arm. "Jack, what do you think you're doing?" he demanded.

I looked at him over the tops of my glasses. "Hunting for a quiet place to talk over our case," I said.

"I thought we were just told to drop it," Nina said, sounding confused.

"We were," I replied. "But if somebody's trying to sabotage the Sail-Off, we have as much right as anybody to try to stop it. We don't need Dave Marsh's permission."

"There's a shady spot," Nina said, pointing. "It's too hot to stand out in the sun."

"Don't you want to work on your tan?" Ollie teased.

"No way," Nina replied. She pulled a plastic tube out of her backpack. "I've been hearing all this stuff about how the sun can really damage your skin, so I try to remember to put sunscreen on whenever I'm outside."

"Hey, can I see that?" I asked, holding out my hand for Nina's sunscreen. I sniffed it, then handed it back. "Nope. Wrong brand."

We sat down on the grass under a big tree. "Here's how I see it," I began. "Dave's flat tires may have been accidents. Even the glued-shut sail bag could have been an accident. But I don't think that suntan lotion got smeared on Dave's wishbone by accident."

"Neither do I," Nina said. Ollie nodded his agreement.

"So that's another dirty trick aimed at Dave, at keeping him from winning the Sail-Off. And no matter what he says, our best suspects are Jason and Freddie, with Sturdevant in third place—only because he doesn't know too much about windsurfing. What now? Do we go on with the case?" I asked them.

"Sure," said Ollie.

"Definitely," Nina agreed. "But how?"

"Good question," I replied. "Any ideas?"

"Maybe we should split up," Ollie suggested. That way, we can each keep an eye on one of the suspects. If any of them tries any more tricks on Dave, we'll catch him at it."

I looked at Nina. "That sounds O.K. to me," she said. "Why don't I take Jason. He paid more attention to you guys than to me when we were questioning him. Maybe he won't notice me."

"O.K.," I agreed. "Ollie, you watch Freddie Ho. I'm pretty sure he saw me listening to his conversation before, but I don't think he noticed you or Nina. And I'll shadow Donald Sturdevant and see what he is up to."

We found Jason down on the beach, standing by his sailboard. He was still wearing his buoyancy belt, which boardsailors use to help keep them afloat if they get injured or knocked out in a wipeout. He was rubbing his hair with a towel. I deduced that he had just come in off the water. He spotted us and called, "Hey, dude, it's Jack B. Quick again! How's your case going?"

Nina, a few feet from me, faded into the crowd.

I shrugged and said, "Dave called it off. He decided it was probably just a series of accidents." Now maybe he'll drop his guard, I thought to myself.

"Yeah," Jason said. "That makes sense. It's too bad though—Dave had a really good shot at winning."

"Speaking of winning," I put in, "how are you doing?"

Jason took off his belt and his wetsuit top. "Great," he replied. "I took a solid first in the speed trials just now. If I can hold my own in the slalom, you'll find me bagging rays on a Hawaiian beach before long."

He picked up a plastic bottle and started smoothing a clear liquid over the tops of his shoulders.

"Is that sunscreen?" I asked.

"Nope, just baby oil," Jason replied. "My skin gets really dry inside the wetsuit sometimes. By the way, Jack, your nose is a little pink. You should be careful. Why don't you ask Dave Marsh for some sunblock? He always buys the strongest he can find. With his coloring, he has to."

"Thanks. I'll do that," I said. "See you later." As I walked off to go look for Sturdevant, I spotted Nina in the middle of a little clump of spectators. We ignored each other.

Freddie Ho was standing near the judges' table, looking over some papers. Ollie was not far away. He nodded slightly as I walked past. I made my way through the crowd, then back again, but I didn't see Sturdevant anywhere.

Finally, I spotted him walking up the path toward the parking lot. I followed at a distance, keeping out of sight as much as I could. Sturdevant paused near a battered red van with a sailboard rack on top. My heart started to pound. Was he about to give Dave another couple of flat tires? But all he did was check his bearings, then head off to the left. A minute later, he stopped by a shiny, powerful-looking sports car, climbed in and drove away. So much for my tailing job!

As I walked back to the beach, I tried to decide on my next move. I was starting to have some ideas about the solution to our mystery, but I didn't see how we were going to prove it. At last, I approached Dave's sailboard and gave it a good look. Then I found a shady place where I could see it and sat myself down.

Out on the waves, a stronger breeze was putting extra zip in the freestyle finals. Each competitor got a chance to do his or her stuff right in front of the judges' table. They were jumping the waves, zipping from one tack to the other, facing outward while holding the sail with arms stretched behind their backs—just about everything except sailing a board while standing on their heads. And there were one or two competitors who looked as though they would like to fit that in, too.

Suddenly I sat up straighter, holding my breath. Somebody in a hat with a wide, floppy brim had just stopped next to Dave's board. I relaxed a little. The guy's back was to me, but I thought I recognized him. He knelt with one knee in the sand and leaned over the board for a few moments. Then he stood up and turned to scan the crowd.

"Freddie," he called. "Hey, dude! Come here a minute!"

Freddie pushed his way through the crowd of spectators. I got to my feet and strolled as close as I could without being conspicuous.

"What's up, Dave?" Freddie asked. "Is there a problem?"

Dave Marsh pushed the floppy hat back from his face and said, "There sure is. I'm dropping out of the Sail-Off. I've had it."

"What?" The Surf Shop's owner looked shocked. "I don't get it. What's wrong?"

"Too many things," Dave replied. He told Freddie about the flats, the sail bag and the grease on his wishbone during the speed trials. "And just now," he added, "I found something like putty stuck in the track of my mast. I think I can clean it out, but not in time for the slalom. So that's it, dude. I withdraw."

"That's terrible," Freddie said. "You're one of the best sailors in the meet. Who would do something like this?"

I glanced around and saw Nina a few feet away. I caught her eye and beckoned with my head. When she joined me, I whispered, "Did you see Freddie go anywhere near Dave's sailboard?"

"No," she whispered back. "He stayed near the judges'

table the whole time. He couldn't have done it."

"We've got to get to the bottom of this," Freddie was saying. "When there is dishonesty in a contest, everybody loses."

"Why not just forget it?" Dave said. He sounded tired. "Somebody has it in for me, that's all. Once I drop out, it will be over."

"We can't just let something like this go by, Dave," Freddie protested. "This affects the other competitors, too. How will they feel if they have to wonder whether they won fair and square? No way around it—we have to find out who's been doing this to you." Freddie glanced over his shoulder. "I wish that little plane would go away. The noise it makes is worse than a cloud of mosquitoes."

Dave looked pale. "Freddie, please," he said. "Do me a favor. Just drop it. There won't be any more dirty tricks. Maybe I imagined the whole thing."

I stepped forward. "No, you didn't, Dave," I said.

Freddie scowled suspiciously. "Who are you?" he demanded.

"This is Jack B. Quick," Dave said reluctantly.

"Oh, sure," said Freddie. "The sports detective."

Pleased to be recognized, I pushed up my glasses and went on. "Dave, you didn't imagine the whole thing. Somebody really did smear slippery goo on your wishbone and stick something in the mast track of your board. And I think I know who it was. What I haven't figured out yet is why."

"Look, dude," said Dave, taking a step in my direction. "I thought I told you to leave it alone."

I stepped back. "You did," I admitted. "But once my friends and I were on the case, we had to see it through to the end. And I think we're just about there."

The spectators were starting to sense that something was going on. As the crowd around us grew, Dave, still talking to Freddie, became more and more uneasy. Maybe he didn't like being hemmed in, or maybe he didn't want everyone to hear about what he had been going through.

I spotted Ollie at the back of the crowd and motioned for him to come forward. Quietly, he reported that Jason had just come back from the ocean. He had spent the whole time practicing and had never come anywhere near Dave's sailboard. In return, I told both Ollie and Nina that Sturdevant had left the meet altogether.

"We're sunk, then," Ollie groaned. "None of our suspects worked out."

"That's because we overlooked the most obvious one," I replied in a low voice. "You know what they say to look for in a criminal investigation—means, opportunity and motive. Who had the best opportunity to monkey with Dave's sailboard, or to flatten his tires? Who had the easiest access to the means of messing him up in the speed trials? For me, the same answer comes up both times. It's—"

"Hey, Jack," Freddie called, breaking off his conversation with Dave. "Can you and your friends really figure out what's been going on here?"

"That's right," I replied. "If I can ask a few questions."

"Go ahead," Freddie invited me. Suddenly, the attention of the entire crowd was on me, Jack B. Quick.

"Dave," I began, after clearing my throat nervously, "do you use sunblock when you're going to be out on the water?"

He frowned, hesitated for a moment, then said, "Sure. I use it even when I'm on the beach. My skin burns easily."

"Do you have it with you? Can I see it?"

Dave groped around in his shoulder bag, found the bottle and tossed it to me. I squeezed some onto my fingertips, rubbed it with my thumb and sniffed. It was thick and greasy and smelled like coconuts.

"When your sail bag was glued shut this morning," I continued, "what kind of glue was it?"

Dave shrugged, glaring at me with obvious dislike. "How should I know?" he said. "It was glue, dude. Clear, with little bubbles, like airplane cement. Glue, that's all."

I saw Jason in the crowd and said to him, "We thought we saw some airplane cement in your pocket earlier today. Is that right?"

"What if it is?" Jason asked with a scowl. "The wrapping on my handgrip was getting loose, and I needed to fasten it down."

"Do you always bring airplane cement to windsurfing meets?"

"When I remember," Jason said. "Today, I forgot, so I borrowed somebody else's. Dave's, to be exact."

"Wrong," Dave said loudly. "I didn't have any. How could I lend you what I didn't have?"

Jason gave him a puzzled look. "I found it in your tool box," he said. "Maybe somebody else left it there."

The crowd began to buzz. Jason had just admitted going through someone else's gear. Who could tell what else he might have done? Jason sensed their reaction and shifted nervously from one foot to the other. "Hey," he said. "Dave and I borrow stuff from each other all the time. Right, dude?"

The pause was just long enough to be noticeable. "Sure, dude. That's right," Dave finally said.

"I didn't put glue on your sail bag," Jason said, with more emphasis. "I couldn't have."

"You could have," I interrupted. "But that's not to say you did. As for the latest dirty trick, I looked at Dave's board less than half an hour ago, and there wasn't anything in the mast track that shouldn't be. After that, I watched carefully. No one—not anyone—came near the board between then and the time Dave discovered the sabotage."

"Impossible!" Freddie exclaimed.

"Is it?" I asked. "Ollie, what do you think?"

Ollie wrinkled his forehead in thought. Then his face cleared. "I get it," he announced. "Only one person could have put the stuff in the mast track. But why—"

"This is ridiculous," Dave cut in loudly. "Don't encourage them, Freddie. I already told you I'm pulling out of the meet."

Freddie looked at Dave, and his expression changed. "They must mean you," he said, incredulously. "Who'd notice if you went over to your own board and started fiddling around with something?"

"What are you—?" Dave began.

"You're the only one who could have done it," I said.

63

"I even saw you lean over the board and do something. Now I realize you were sticking something in the mast track. But why? Why sabotage your own performance?"

I gazed out to sea, looking for inspiration. A few sailboards were tacking back and forth, their sails colorful in the afternoon sun. Farther out over the water, the ultra-light plane flew past at about the speed of a car in heavy traffic.

A lightbulb went on in my brain. I stepped up close to Dave and said softly, "Don't you want to win a round-trip airplane ticket to Hawaii?"

Dave stared at me, stunned. He reached over and pushed me away. I turned to Freddie. "I think we'd better finish this in private," I said.

A few minutes later, in a roped off area behind the judges' table, I explained. "Dave must suffer from an airplane phobia, an intense fear of flying," I began. "He couldn't bear the thought of flying to Hawaii—all those hours in the air—but he couldn't bear destroying his reputation by deliberately doing poorly and losing the meet. So he pretended to be the victim of sabotage instead."

"Then he brought us in to make his story more believable," Ollie said.

"Right," I agreed. "But we started coming too close to his secret, so he tried to pull us off the case."

I paused, then added, "I should have figured it out earlier. Every time that ultra-light plane flew by, Dave almost fainted, but there was always some other explanation. And every time we started to build a case against a subject, he got very upset. He didn't want anyone else to be blamed for what he was doing."

Jason went over and clapped Dave on the back. "I wish you'd told me, dude," he said. "Is that why you took the train to that contest in California? I would have gone with you if I'd known. I'm not so hot about flying myself." The two of them walked down the beach toward Jason's sailboard.

"You know, if Dave had just decided to give the ticket to the *dude* who won second place, none of this would have happened," Nina commented, as we watched Dave and Jason walk away.

"Yeah," Ollie agreed. "But it could have been a lot worse. Dave might have hurt himself—or completely ruined the Sail-Off for everyone."

"That's true. At least we caught him before Freddie called it off," I added. "And maybe now Dave will find someone to help him get over his fear of flying. Come on, dudes. Let's go see who's winning the volleyball match."

Case closed.

The Case
of the
Unset Nets

"Hey, check it out!" exclaimed Ollie to Nina and me. "It looks like a funeral march!"

Nina and I looked up the hill where Johnson Junior High's tennis courts are located. The entire tennis team was walking slowly toward us, heads down and rackets dragging. I checked my digital watch and noticed that it was only 3:05. If my memory served me correctly—and it usually does, since keeping track of facts is a very important part of my job as Jack B. Quick, sports detective—practice had only started at 2:50. How could it possibly be over so early?

"Yo, Jack, am I glad to see you," called Tim Newton, the captain of the tennis team, as he and his teammates approached us. "We've got a problem," he continued, running a hand distractedly through his sandy-blond hair as he stopped in front of me.

"Hi, Tim," I greeted him with a huge smile. I always get excited when I smell a new case. I can't help it. It's kind

66

of like starting a book you know is going to be great. "Does your problem have something to do with why you've been ending practice early? Didn't you also have to cut things short just two days ago?"

Tim's blue eyes studied me seriously. "Jack B. Quick, you just hit the nail on the head," he replied. "Our practices have been cut down—literally. Someone has been stealing our tennis nets so we can't practice at all anymore. When the first set was stolen, we put up the spares. Now they're gone, too. If this keeps up, we won't have a prayer of holding our own this season."

"Sounds like the work of the Toughs," Nina offered, scuffing the toe of her penny loafer against the grass impatiently and looking from me to Tim. Nina is a high-energy kind of person and she likes to get down to business right away. Her get-up-and-go personality makes her an invaluable associate and member of the Jack B. Quick Detective Squad.

"The *who*?" Ollie asked, running a hand across his hair, which is cut in a high-top fade, a confused expression on his face.

"No, they're a rock band," I pointed out with a laugh. I can't resist pulling Ollie's chain once in a while. He's not exactly up on classic rock and roll like I am, and I know almost nothing about the hip-hop house music he loves. Despite our musical differences, the two of us have been friends forever and he's been my associate almost as long as I've been in business.

"Very funny," Nina commented, snapping her bubble

gum and staring at me as if I had two heads or something. Sometimes Nina has no sense of humor at all. "The Toughs are a gang of high school kids who have been going around to lots of junior highs and wrecking all kinds of stuff. They're real jerks, but they're very crafty. No one has been able to lay a finger on them so far."

"We may have to play tough on this one, you guys," I said in my serious detective voice. "Say, Tim, do you think we can talk to the rest of the team now to try and pick up some clues?"

"Sure, Jack, no problem," Tim assured me. "Everyone's here except Skip Lewis. He said he was going to go play tennis at his mother's club."

"Really?" I said, shooting up my eyebrows. How high I raise my eyebrows above my glasses is a good indication of my interest level.

"Yeah, he's the only one lucky enough to still have a court to play on. If this net stealing keeps up, Skip may turn out to be our only player worth his weight on the court this season."

Nina and Ollie both looked at me. I knew what they were thinking without being told because I was sure it had to be exactly what I was thinking—we would have to check out this Skip character as soon as possible. It sounded as if he might be our very first suspect in what I had come to think of as *The Case of the Unset Nets*. But first things first.

"Nina, Ollie, let's go visit the scene of the crime," I suggested. "I want to search for any evidence we can find." This was going to be an interesting case. I could taste it already—the same way you know how a triple-thick choco-late shake is going to be even before it hits your mouth.

We said good-bye to Tim and told him we would be in touch. Then the three of us hiked up to the courts. We stood there for a minute just looking at the green hard courts. Tim was right. There was not a net to be seen anywhere.

"Wow!" exclaimed Ollie. "What could have happened to all the nets?"

"This is serious stuff, you guys," added Nina. "Some-body is going to a whole lot of trouble to make these courts unplayable."

Ollie and Nina looked to me for answers. I didn't have any—not just then anyway. The three of us inspected each court carefully, but there was not a shred of evidence of any sort to be found anywhere. I could tell it was going to be one of those cases—the tough kind (no pun intended).

The next day at school, I cut out of lunch a little early to visit my friend Nancy, the co-editor-in-chief of the Johnson Junior High newspaper, in the school's newspaper office. Because I write for the paper, I know Nancy pretty well even though she's in ninth grade. She trained the other editor, Kris Hanning, a seventh grader who had helped me on an earlier case. Ollie's always teasing me about having a crush on her, but I don't, of course. We're just business friends—that's all.

"Hey, Nance, what's up?" I greeted her as I walked into the deserted newspaper office.

"Well, if it isn't the famous Jack B. Quick!" Nancy exclaimed. "I haven't seen you around for quite a while.

What can I do for you?" she asked with a smile.

"What makes you think I want something done, Nancy?" I retorted immediately. Then, exactly what I dreaded might happen, happened—I blushed. Nancy has that effect on me sometimes—not that Ollie's right about my having a crush on her or anything, but there's something about her long blonde hair and big brown eyes. . . .

"Listen, Jack, I know you well enough by now. Out with it! What super-duper case are you trying to crack now?" Nancy demanded.

I told her about the mysterious disappearance of the school's tennis nets. I wanted to check the sports pages of the newspaper for the tennis match results of the last few seasons. There was a vague inkling of a clue hanging around the cobwebs in the back of my brain, and I figured the paper just might hold the key.

Nancy motioned toward the files at the back of the room and I began to go through past issues of *The Eagle*, our school newspaper. All the tennis articles were pretty straightforward until I got to one from two years earlier that proved to be quite interesting. My detective's intuition had done its work again.

"Ah-ha!" I yelled. "I knew I remembered something rumored about foul play during the tennis season two years ago."

"Oh, you mean with Whitman Junior High winning the county championships?" offered Nancy matter-of-factly with a toss of her long blonde hair.

"Exactly, Nancerooney!" I replied, pushing my glasses

70

up farther on my nose and walking over to her desk, the issue of *The Eagle* in question clutched tightly in my hand. "Whitman had consistently beaten us for four straight years, and then during that season two years ago, it just didn't have as strong a team. We beat Whitman once during the regular season, and then our second match was canceled on account of rain. Since the rain-out was near the end of our regular season, we never made up the match. By the time the post-season tourney started, the Whitman players were pretty psyched out by our team."

"Enough to go to extracurricular extremes to win?" asked Nancy.

"Precisely!" I replied, pacing the floor in front of her desk. I pace a lot when I'm in the middle of something—it helps me think. "It seems that a Whitman player, Jim Starr, actually cut the strings on some of the Johnson players' tennis rackets in order to gain an unfair advantage," I continued. "What he didn't know was that all our players have extra rackets that the team manager carries in a separate bag for the occasional broken string or unraveled grip. Anyway, we won the counties that year, and Starr was discovered and banned from the first half of the following year's season."

"You think that *he* stole our nets, Jack?" Nancy asked, her brown eyes widening with concern.

"Let me just say that I wouldn't put it past him, Nance," I replied evenly. "Thanks for the research materials! I've got to run."

With a quick wave, I was out of the newspaper office, my mind churning with the first real hard evidence of the case. The truth is that I could have talked to Nancy all day. I find her, well, to put it quite simply . . . cute. But at the moment, work had to be done, so I high-tailed it down the hall to science class. We were supposed to start dissecting frogs and I have to admit that I wasn't exactly looking forward to it. Nina loves that sort of thing, but I think it's kind of disgusting. Taking apart engines is one thing, but animals—that's an entirely different story. It's a little on the barbaric side if you ask me, not that anyone was. At least we didn't have to dissect a pig or a cat.

I made it through science class O.K. We ended up spending the entire period discussing *how* to dissect without actually doing the dissection, which was fine with me. Then I had a quiz in social studies about the American Revolution, which happens to be my favorite subject. I knew as soon as I had finished that I had aced it. I have a great memory for dates.

I walked down the hall toward my locker and started thinking about the missing tennis nets again. I had put the case out of my mind since I'd chatted with Nancy in the newspaper office.

"Yo, Jack!" Ollie called to me from down the hall. "Where are you off to, dude?"

"Ollie, grab your bike," I replied quickly. "We're headed for a little tennis practice."

"We're going to play tennis?" Ollie asked with a frown. An all-around athlete, tennis is one of the few sports Ollie doesn't really like.

"No, we're going to watch some tennis over at Whitman Junior High," I explained patiently. "I'm curious about Whitman's team this year, that's all."

"Yeah, right, Jack," Ollie commented, shifting his black, yellow and neon-green nylon knapsack from one shoulder to the other as he stared at me. "Come on, what's really up?"

I gave Ollie a brief outline of what I had discovered in the newspaper office. I didn't want to tell him anything too specific because he tends to jump to conclusions. I wanted him to have as open a mind about this as possible. "Let's go."

Ollie and I biked over to the Whitman tennis courts and found the team warming up with jumping jacks on the center court. "One . . . and two . . . and three . . . and four . . . and one . . . and two . . ." shouted their coach, Mr. Sanders.

"Which one's Starr?" asked Ollie.

"That's him on the end," I explained, pointing to a tall kid with curly brown hair who was wearing a black concert T-shirt and a pair of white tennis shorts with black biker shorts underneath. "That's our Jim Starr all right."

"He looks like a pretty cool guy to me, Jack," Ollie commented. "You sure he messed with those rackets two years ago?"

"I only know what the record says, Ollie," I replied. "I'd like to talk to him to see if he knows anything about our missing nets. I guess we'll have to wait until practice is over."

Two hours later, with the afternoon sun burning red just above the horizon, the sweaty tennis players we had been

73

watching so avidly finally began their cool-down jog along the path to the locker room and showers. "Excuse me, Jim Starr!" I called as the curly-headed kid ran past. He looked over at me in surprise and then walked toward Ollie and me.

"Yeah, I'm Jim Starr," he said. "What's up? And who are you?"

"I'm Jack B. Quick, sports detective, and this is my colleague, Ollie Steele," I replied smoothly.

Starr gave me an obnoxious smirk and squinted his green eyes into mean slits. It didn't faze me, though. It's common among suspects to be suspicious of detectives, so I'm used to dealing with this sort of behavior. "Let me guess," Starr finally said, still smirking. "Somebody's messing around with something and you just want to ask me a few questions."

"Uh, that's correct," I replied, a bit taken aback by his directness. He was clearly not a beating-around-the-bush kind of guy.

"Look, Mr. Detective, I know that I have a reputation because of what happened two years ago, but let me set the record straight," Starr spat out. "I was a confused little punk back then, but I don't do stuff like that anymore. I learned my lesson big time. Anyway, what would I do with a bunch of tennis nets?"

With that, Starr ran off before I could even open my mouth to answer him. "Strange," I remarked to Ollie. "I never even mentioned the stolen nets to him."

"That's right!" Ollie exclaimed, scratching his head.

The sun was beginning to set, so we quickly hopped on

our bikes and headed for home. I had been meaning to install a new head lamp on my bike for a while. It was just one of those things that you keep putting off because you are too busy hanging out with your friends, or going to the movies or, as in my case (sorry, no pun intended), solving sports mysteries. Anyway, I wished I had installed that light because as Ollie and I rode down Elm Street back to our town, it started to get dark and I couldn't see nearly as well as I would have liked. I was hoping that Ollie could see better than I could because I was following him about ten bike lengths behind.

"Yowza!" screamed Ollie, as he swerved his bike wildly out into the middle of the street. Ollie never acts foolishly on a bicycle, so I knew there had to be a good reason for this crazy riding. Just then, I saw the reason for myself.

At one of the side streets that runs into Elm, a noisy, rumbling black Volkswagen bug was stopped. (VW bugs, in case you didn't know, are those little cars that were really popular back in the '60s, and because they're hard to find now, they're considered cool.) The car's front bumper was sticking way out into the street where it definitely should not have been.

As I swerved around it, I tried to get a good look at the driver. I wanted to at least give him my evil eye and let him know I was annoyed at his unsafe driving practices. I couldn't get a good look at anybody in the car, however. But I did catch a glimpse of a large red "T" painted inside a red square on the driver's door.

"You O.K., Ollie?" I shouted ahead.

"Yeah, fine . . . just a little surprised," he called back.

"Whoever is driving that thing should be . . . " My words were drowned out by an ear-splitting rumble directly behind me. The evil black car was right on my tail!

"Pedal faster, Ollie," I cried as I pumped my legs furiously up and down, trying to get my old ten-speed to move. Ollie actually stood up on his pedals and really started to fly. I made sure to stick right behind him even though I was breathing so hard my glasses began to fog up a little.

"Beeeeeeeeeeeeeep!!!" Whoever was in the VW bug honked the horn for about five seconds straight. The sound boomed in my eardrums like a cannon.

I noticed that there was a stoplight up ahead where Pacific Boulevard crosses Elm Street. A stoplight! I prayed for a green light for Ollie and me and a big fat red light for the jerks behind us. No chance. The light turned red long before we reached it. Ollie stopped and I stopped right behind him. Just then, the rumbling monster pulled up alongside of us. I gulped. I felt as if we were in a chase scene right out of the movies. The front window on the passenger side was slowly rolled down and a kid with a ton of black hair on his head leaned out of the window and leered at us.

"Hey, that wasn't too cool back there," I stammered, trying to sound a lot more confident than I felt.

"Chill out, you four-eyed detective!" returned the hairy kid in the car. As I peered more closely, I could see that the tiny car was filled with several kids with just as much hair. There were five of them, in fact. Two sat in the front and three were squished together in the back. The hairy kid in front continued to stare at us, his scrawny arm dangling along the side of the front door. I noticed that he had a tatoo on his forearm—a capital letter "T" in a red square.

"Why don't you leave us alone!" Ollie suddenly bellowed in a deep voice I hadn't known he possessed. Leave it to Ollie—the guy was always surprising me.

"Leave you alone?!" the hair-mop said with another leer. "You're in our neck of the woods, boys . . . you're in 'Tough Territory.' " All the kids in the car started laughing. "Stay in your own town if you know what's good for you!" he added.

Just then, the light turned green. Ollie crossed Pacific and took a sharp right onto Maple Avenue at the next intersection. I followed like a robot. We pedaled at top speed for another five minutes and then I started to slow down. Everything was quiet and the VW bug was nowhere in sight.

"It's O.K., Ollie, slow down," I yelled. He kept pedaling without looking back once. I saw him turn off at his house and I figured that, since it was late, I ought to be heading home myself. Ollie and I would just have to perform a slow-motion replay of this scene at a later time.

After school the next day, I stopped by to see Nancy at the newspaper office—on business, of course. I told her in gruesome detail about my heroic brush with death the night before.

"But why would they feel threatened by you being in their territory?" Nancy wanted to know. "I mean, no offense, Jack, but you don't exactly look like the threatening type."

"We-ell, Nancy," I began to explain, my voice inconveniently cracking, "I think they felt threatened because they thought I was closing in on a clue—a clue that would lead to them."

"But how did they know who you were . . . that you weren't just some kid on a bike?" Nancy asked immediately.

"Gee, I don't know, Nancy," I replied in my most humble of voices. "I guess my fame has started to spread across the state, that's all. Anyway, Nina suspected that the Toughs had something to do with the stolen nets right from the beginning. Do we have any dirt on them? That's really why I stopped by."

Nancy went over to her computer. She had created a database to store everything the school newspaper had covered over the past two years, an invaluable source of information for my cases.

"Toughs . . . Toughs . . . Toughs . . . " muttered Nancy as she searched her files. "Tough-minded Social Studies teacher . . . no . . . tough luck for fencing team . . . no . . . ah, here we are: Toughs, The . . . see issue of November 3."

Nancy flipped off the computer and led me to a bookcase that went all the way from the floor straight to the ceiling. She pulled out an eight-inch-thick binder and opened it. We found the November third issue without a problem, and, sure enough, on page six there was a short article about school vandalism.

I skimmed the article quickly with Nancy reading over my shoulder. I noticed that she smelled good—kind of like peppermint candy. The article was pretty straightforward and not very insightful until we got to the fourth paragraph:

"One of the more disturbing acts of vandalism in local schools is something that goes beyond mere pranksterism. And that is deliberate destruction of school property. Such was the case recently at Whitman Junior High, where the pool lane markers were slashed to pieces and rendered completely unusable. The group responsible for this action is known as the Toughs. In this reporter's opinion they would be more aptly named the Losers.

"This group of trouble-making high school students participate in no school activity themselves, but instead spend their ample free time making life more difficult for those students who are busy bettering themselves and their community.

"The members of the Toughs appear only with fellow group members. They often use intimidation to get their way. And they often do get their way, namely because of their numbers. To break up this group, we must go to the families because . . ."

I had read enough. It seemed pretty clear to me that the Toughs could easily have stolen the tennis nets. Their motive? Simply to be mean, that's it. I knew from past experience that crimes like this were the hardest to solve because it was so difficult to prove anything.

"So, what do you think, Jack?" Nancy asked, breaking my train of thought.

I looked up and found myself gazing right into her brown eyes. "I . . . uh . . . think I gotta go now, Nance. Thanks a lot for your help," I blurted out. My pulse was racing as I left the newspaper office. I told myself it was because of this case—it had nothing to do with Nancy.

"There he is—there's the guy who told off the Toughs!" a voice yelled. It was Ollie. Students up and down the halls stopped what they were doing and stared at me.

"No, no, no, Oliver," I returned with a grin. "I believe you were the one who told off the Toughs!"

By then, a small crowd had gathered around us. Ollie and I stage these mock arguments every so often just to attract attention and shake things up a little bit. Sometimes people come up to us afterward with information on the case we were "arguing" about. Besides, it's great publicity for the Jack B. Quick Detective Squad.

"I'm telling you, as sure as my name is Oliver Randolph Steele, I witnessed this mild-mannered student of our beloved Johnson Junior High, Mr. Jack B. Quick, as he reckoned with one of the meanest, ugliest, toughest of the Toughs!"

"Well, you're right on one count, Ollie," I said. "He was ugly." This got some mega-laughs out of the group of students crowded around us.

"Where did you run into them?" somebody asked.

"Well, like I said, it was night and pitch black out. Jack and I were riding down Elm Street near the Pacific Boulevard light, when all of a sudden, completely out of nowhere, there appeared this evil black—black as the night—car!"

There was a gasp as the spectators in the hall drew in their breath. I had to admit that Ollie was painting the picture quite well. I often tell him he should be on the stage.

"I couldn't see anybody inside the car," Ollie continued in the same dramatic tone. "It moved as if a ghost was driving it. Then, all of a sudden, it shot out of a side street toward me. I swerved into the middle of the road on my bike to avoid being crushed by its hungry tires of death!"

The hallway erupted into a chorus of "oohs" and "ahs" at Ollie's grand finale. Just then, the piercing sound of the late bell echoed through the corridor. Most of the kids visibly jumped, startled by the sound.

"To be continued next period, same place!" shouted Ollie as his audience scattered, trying to make it to class on time. Ollie winked at me and I waved back before I took off for English class.

I was the last one in my seat. "As I was saying," continued Mr. Wright, my English teacher, "*Huckleberry Finn* is more than just the story of a boy's adventure—"

Suddenly, the classroom door burst open and one of the secretaries from the school office walked inside. She handed Mr. Wright a note and before I knew what was happening, I was following the secretary out of the classroom. I felt myself blushing because, although I knew I hadn't done anything wrong, I also knew that that was what everyone else in the class was thinking.

The secretary told me in a less than friendly tone that Coach Peterson wanted to see me and then she turned and walked back to the office. Had I done something wrong? Was I short any gym credits? I had no clue why in the world Coach Peterson would want to see me. I mean, I might not be the most athletic guy in the world, but I always try my hardest in gym. I took a deep breath and knocked on the frosted window of the coach's office.

"Come on in," he called. Coach Peterson was sitting behind his desk with his sneakered feet propped up in front of him. I noticed that he was reading the current issue of *World Tennis*.

"Hi ya, Jack, have a seat," Coach said quickly. A tanned former All-America tennis player, Coach Peterson had come to Johnson just last year from a small junior high school in California. He coached our school tennis team and taught paddleball and golf in gym class. He was a very easygoing coach, a quality that I attributed to the California influence.

"Hi, Coach Peterson, anything wrong?" I asked, getting right to the point. Despite his friendly attitude, I still feared I had done something wrong because he had called me out of a class.

"Yes, Jack, something is wrong, very wrong," the coach replied, a frown crossing his tanned features. Oh boy, I thought, bracing myself for the reprimand.

"As you know, someone has been stealing the nets up at our tennis courts," the coach continued gravely.

So, this was a business call. I quickly changed gears, taking off my imaginary scared-student hat and putting on my official Jack B. Quick sports detective hat. "Yes, Coach, I am well aware of the problem. In fact, your team captain, Tim Newton, has already asked me to look into the mystery."

"Tim told me that you were working on the case and I wanted to thank you for your time," Coach went on. "I thought it would be beneficial if you and I had a talk about the situation in hopes that we might turn up a clue or two. I apologize for pulling you out of class, Jack, but you can understand that I'm quite upset about these stolen nets. They're very expensive to replace and we've already lost two sets of nets. I'm afraid to install another set because I think we'll just keep losing them until we find out who's running away with them."

"I agree, Coach," I answered immediately. "I already have a couple of suspects in mind, so it shouldn't be too long before we find out who has been running off with your nets."

Just then, we were interrupted by a knock on the door.

"Come on in," Coach Peterson called in the same friendly voice he had used for me. That friendliness was a very good character trait because it made you feel as if you could come and talk to him at any time. I made a mental note about this because I admired it. I would have to incorporate it into my personality so that I could use it when I was in a position of authority.

Stan Musacs, one of the key players on the tennis team and a really nice guy, walked inside. "Hey, Coach . . . hey, Jack, what are you doing here?" he said.

"Just getting some tennis pointers, Stan," I replied smoothly. In my line of work, I have learned that it is vital to be able to come up with white lies on the spot when it's necessary. "How are you doing?"

"Oh, I'm all right, I guess," Stan said, "despite the fact that we haven't had a practice for days now. I wonder if I'll even remember how to serve when I play again."

"You better remember how to serve, Musacs," Coach

83

commented. "We're counting on you. We're still playing our opening match against Jefferson this Friday. I thought everyone knew that."

"No, just the opposite, Coach," Stan replied. "I was hearing rumors that all our matches were going to be canceled!"

"Canceled?! That's crazy!" Coach retorted. "You guys are too talented to waste an entire season over some missing nets. Start spreading the word with the team, would you, Stan?"

"Will do, Coach," Stan said. "Will there be practice after school today?"

"You bet," Coach Peterson said with a smile. "We may not have our nets but you guys still have your legs. We're going to do some conditioning drills."

After Stan had left the office, Coach Peterson turned back to me. "Where were we, Jack?" he asked.

"I was telling you about my suspects, Coach," I replied. "First of all, there's this guy over at Whitman by the name of Jim Starr."

"Say no more, Jack," the coach responded. "I remember hearing that story about him from two years ago. Is he still around?"

"Yeah, he goes on to high school next year," I answered. "Anyway, he seemed to know an awful lot about the missing nets for a guy who lives two towns away. I also have suspicions about that group called the Toughs. This is just the kind of vandalism that gives them their jollies. I have to talk to some more people, though, before I take these hunches any further. I've also been meaning to talk to one of your players, Coach."

"You think that someone on *my* team would want to steal our nets?" Coach sputtered in surprise. "Jack, I have great admiration for your work, but with all due respect, isn't that a little ridiculous?"

"Believe me, Coach, weirder things have happened before," I said calmly. "As a detective, I have trained myself not to ignore what may seem entirely implausible on the outside. If you do that, you take the chance of passing up something that may be lurking below the surface—some little nugget of truth that can hold the key to solving a case."

"I see," said the coach after a long pause.

"I just wanted to talk to Skip Lewis for a few minutes," I explained. "Tim was telling me that through these missed practices, Skip has been the only team member able to continue practicing because his mother belongs to a tennis club and has access to a court. Now, that's a possible motive right there. Skip may have orchestrated this net disappearance so that he would be the only player able to continue practicing. Therefore, he would be the only player actually able to improve his playing while everyone else on the team, if anything, only got worse. That's undoubtedly one way to achieve the number one position."

"Jack B. Quick, you have a devious mind," announced Coach Peterson, swinging his legs off his desk to the floor and staring at me closely.

"You have to think deviously if you want to get inside the mind of someone who does wrong, Coach," I replied grimly. At that moment there was a loud knock at the door.

"Come on in," said Coach Peterson. Robert Marks rushed into the office, his face flushed red. Our tennis team's Number 1 singles and doubles player, Robert is a very talented athlete, but he is also one of the worst-tempered, most spoiled players you would ever want to meet. In other words—he is good and he knows it.

Without even a hello, Robert launched into a loud and obnoxious tirade. "The Jefferson match is on?!" he huffed. "How can we possibly compete, Coach? By the time of the match, we won't have had a single practice in over a week."

"Hello to you too, Mr. Marks," replied Coach Peterson calmly. "We will play Jefferson because I think you men are ready for it. It's that simple."

"Well, I am not playing doubles with Smith—no way!" Robert shot back. "That guy will make me look like a turkey, I just know it."

"Robert, since when do we put our own interests above the interests of the team?" Coach Peterson demanded, impressing me with his composure in the face of the out of control and out of line Robert. "You will be playing Number 1 singles and then doubles with Don Smith and I am sure that you will play well together. You complement each other's strengths and weaknesses quite nicely."

"He'll get no compliments from me!" yelled Robert as he stormed out of the office.

"Just a little pre-match nerves, Jack," Coach said. "Don't pay attention to him. You know how high-strung some really talented players can be. Look at John McEnroe."

I left Coach Peterson's office with more questions in my head than when I had entered. *The Case of the Unset Nets* was getting tangled indeed.

I hurried to my locker to get my social studies book and notebook. As soon as I opened it, I noticed a folded piece of paper lying on top of my books. Someone must have stuck the note through the vent slots. I unfolded the piece of paper and felt as if I had been punched in the stomach. I just stood there without moving for a few seconds, staring at the paper in my hand.

"Hey, Jack, you look like you just saw a ghost," announced Nancy, shifting her books from one arm to the other and staring at me in concern.

"Yeah, a ghost," I croaked. "My own."

Before I could say another word, Nancy had taken the piece of paper out of my clenched hand.

"Jack, look at your hand . . . it's bleeding!" Nancy cried.

"Wh-what?" I said. "Oh, no, that's not blood. I guess the red ink from the note must have rubbed off on me. Go ahead and read it."

" 'Mind your own business. Or else!' " Nancy read aloud. "And it's signed with a big red capital 'T.' Jack, who is this? What have you gotten into?"

"Nancy, it's a long story," I replied, secretly pleased by her overt display of concern for my safety and well-being. "I have to get to class now, but I promise I'll stop by and fill you in later, O.K.?"

"Well, O.K.," she replied with a little smile.

I walked quickly to class. I had to get away from Nancy

87

before she saw just how spooked I really was. Things rarely throw me off the way that note had, but honestly, it gave me goosebumps just thinking about it. O.K., Jack, I thought, act calm, be calm, think calm. Everything's fine . . . That's what I always tell myself when I begin to panic.

I sat in social studies class and listened very carefully to Mrs. Jacobs's lecture on the Lewis and Clark expedition, but I don't actually think I heard a single word of it.

I rushed out of Mrs. Jacobs's classroom at the end of the period to tell Ollie about the note in my locker. He agreed that we had to do something—and fast.

After school, Ollie and I hopped on our bikes and rode over to the Maple Tennis Club, where Skip Lewis's mother had a membership and where we hoped to find Skip. About two blocks from the club, I jammed on my brakes. Ollie nearly slammed into me, but he managed to skid to a stop.

"Over there, Ollie!" I whispered, pointing ahead to a car crossing the street at a slow cruising speed. It was the black Volkswagen with the big red "T" painted on the side.

"We can't seem to steer clear of them, can we?" Ollie said.

"Ollie, the question is whether this is an accident or whether they are after us. I mean, don't forget about that note in my locker. Do you think they're going to mow us down in broad daylight, or what?" I stammered a little, trying to remain calm. I must admit that I am never exactly psyched about physical confrontations.

"Jack, get a grip," Ollie replied, grabbing my shoulder. "This is just a coincidence. Let's get to the club!"

Inside the Maple Tennis Club, the "thwop-thwop" sound of tennis balls being hit reverberated off the walls. Ollie and I stood at the window in the club shop overlooking the 12 courts, searching for Skip. We couldn't see him anywhere. Suddenly, I felt a hard object sticking into the small of my back. Uh-oh, I thought, have the Toughs managed to track us down? Was this about to be the end of my all-too-short life?

"Hey, guys, what's up?" said Skip Lewis, as he pulled the end of his racket away from my back.

"Lewis, you better watch that weapon of yours," I replied. "Somebody could get hurt."

"Hey, Jack, chill out," Skip said with a laugh. "I was only kidding around."

"Well, Skip, I gotta admit that I was a little startled, too," added Ollie.

Skip just shrugged, looking at us as if we were both crazy. He, of course, knew nothing of the note or our most recent encounter with the Toughs. "What are you guys doing here anyway? Want to play a few games?"

"Uh, no thanks, Skip, I'm not dressed for it," I responded. "Actually, we just want to talk to you for a few minutes."

"About the missing tennis nets," Ollie said.

"O.K.," Skip replied pleasantly. "I don't have my court for another fifteen minutes."

Skip proved to be genuinely concerned about the school's missing nets. He felt bad about being the only one on the team able to continue practicing. Originally, he had hoped to bring some of his teammates to the club but according to the rules, members could only have two guests a week. That would put Skip in a tough position.

While Skip had looked like a solid suspect on paper, I became convinced of his innocence after talking to him. I consider myself an extremely good judge of character, so if he was lying, he was doing an excellent job of it. Ollie and I called it a day.

My dad had gotten home early from work, so he made spaghetti and meatballs for dinner—my favorite. After seconds and thirds, I went upstairs to my room to do my homework. I didn't sleep well that night. I dreamed about these weird fishermen who kept throwing their nets overboard into the sea and pulling them up filled with little black Volkswagens. This case obviously needed some serious solving.

The next morning, as I was rushing down the hall to class, I ran headfirst into Robert Marks from the tennis team. "Sorry!" I exclaimed, knowing Robert's short temper all to well.

"No, I'm sorry, Jack, it was my fault," Robert said apologetically. "And I want to apologize to you for busting in on your conversation with Coach Peterson yesterday. I was just a little worked up, that's all," he added, brushing his long dark hair out of his eyes. As his right hand crossed his face, I happened to notice that his index finger, middle finger and thumb were pink at the tips.

"Uh, Robert, have you been eating pistachio nuts lately?" I asked in my friendliest chatty voice.

Robert curled his fingers into a ball and looked visibly frustrated. "Pistachio nuts? No . . . I mean, yeah, that's right I did eat a whole bunch of pistachio nuts the other day. Hey, gotta go!" he concluded as he turned quickly and scooted away. Just then, I spotted Ollie farther down the hall.

"Hey, Ollie!" I yelled.

"Yo, Jack, what's up?" he yelled back.

"Meet me in Coach Peterson's office as soon as the first lunch bell sounds, O.K.?" I asked.

"Gee, Jack, I'm really hungry today," Ollie said grumpily.

"Look, Ol, your stomach can wait, you old Hoover," I retorted. "What I have to reveal will satisfy you like no school lunch ever could!"

"Jack, you know who stole the nets?" Ollie suddenly blurted.

"In a word, yes," I replied mysteriously. "Be there!"

I arrived at Coach Peterson's office at precisely 11:53 that morning. Ollie was already there, waiting. "So, Jack, Ollie tells me you have some news for me," Coach Peterson said.

"I do indeed, Coach," I replied. "Could you please summon Robert Marks to your office?"

Ten minutes later Robert appeared. His confession followed right on the heels of my accusation. "I'm, I'm so so-sorry for this whole me-mess," moaned Robert. "Everybody told me that I was the best and I just didn't want to let them down—my parents, the high school coaches, all the kids at school. When I found out I would be playing doubles with Don Smith, I got . . . scared that I wouldn't be able to play well and that we might actually lose. I thought the season would be canceled if we didn't have nets for the courts. It was the only thing I could do!"

Poor Robert. He actually had tears in his eyes. The pressure of being Number 1 had just been too much for him. I had seen this before. The lengths that people would go to in order to win never ceased to sadden and amaze me.

Coach Peterson put an arm around Robert's shoulder. "I just wanted to be the best. . . . " sobbed Robert.

"Maybe you two should leave us alone for a while," Coach Peterson said softly. On cue, Ollie and I made our exit.

Later that day at the newspaper office, I held court. Ten kids stood around me as I described every step of this most baffling case. "And then what did you do?" somebody asked.

"Wow!" exclaimed another.

"What I don't get is how you got your final clue," Ollie wondered. "The one that pointed the finger at Marks."

"Well, Ollie, it started with the note I found in my locker. I thought it was from the Toughs. When I gave it to Nancy my hand was red from the ink used on the paper," I explained. "It ran when it met the sweat on my hand."

"Yeah," Ollie said. "Go on."

"So, anyway, when I bumped into Robert early the next morning, he brushed his hand across his forehead and I noticed that three of the fingers on his right hand were pink on the pads. It all came together after that. Robert clearly must have known that we had had a run-in with the Toughs—Ollie and I told everybody about it the other day in the hallway—so he took advantage of that fact to direct even more evidence against them."

"You mean that Robert wrote the note from the Toughs?" Nancy asked in surprise.

"Yes, Nancy," I replied with a smile. "I can see that your reporter's instinct is kicking in really strong."

"Just for that crack, Jack B. Quick, I may not take you out for that *T*-bone steak, or give you that special *T*-shirt I had in mind or even build you that *Tee*-pee either," Nancy said with a flip of her long blonde hair.

"O.K., O.K., I get it already," I retorted. "Let's just forget the letter 'T' and the Toughs and the missing nets and go get some chocolate shakes, all right?"

"Now you're talking," Ollie said as a bunch of us took off to get ice cream at Kreagle's. Case closed.

The Case
of the
Lucky Lady

"Ooomph!" I exclaimed as I slammed into the outfield fence. While I watched yet another ball take off over my head for Venus, I wondered why I had ever let my best friend and one of my associates, Ollie Steele, talk me into playing summer league baseball. I have enough to do solving mysteries as Jack B. Quick, sports detective. Besides, I'm not exactly the greatest baseball player in the world, although I really love everything about the sport.

At this moment, though, I was Jack B. Quick, rightfielder for the Kreagle Icemen. We were 1-4 for the season—about to be 1-5. The Howland Pharmacy Eagles were running us into the ground, 6-0. Mr. Kreagle, our team sponsor, had offered to give us all sundaes—for free—after each win. We hadn't tasted victory, or ice cream, in quite some time.

While I waited for another ball to come my way, I tried to guess what my next case would be like. Something to do with swimming, I hoped, something cool. I lifted my cap and wiped the sweat off my face. It was right about then that I noticed the dog.

I don't think anyone really saw where she came from. Suddenly, she was just there, trotting slowly across the infield.

"Hey!" Joey Mehta shouted from his position at shortstop. "Who let that dog on the field?"

Her coat was so dirty it was impossible to tell what color she really was, but I guessed that she was part Labrador retriever. I wasn't sure about the rest—except the part that was pure baseball fan. This dog wanted to get in on the game. She ran up to Joey and tugged at his shoelaces with her teeth. When he tried to grab her worn leather collar, she bounded away, barking.

"Come here, girl!" Nick Klein called from leftfield. The dog ran toward him. Nick has two dogs of his own, so if anybody had a chance of catching this crazy mutt, Nick did. He knelt down beside her and started scratching her behind the ears. Everyone was yelling at Nick to get the dog off the field, but he couldn't grab her collar quickly enough.

Two minutes later, the entire infield was chasing the dog. It was a lot more entertaining than our baseball game, that was for sure. Finally, Don Roberts, our coach, got hold of the playful mutt and led her back to the bench.

He told her to sit and, to my surprise, she did. Then the game started up again, and the Eagles got two more runs to put us down, 8-0.

"Come on, you guys," Coach Roberts called, clapping

his hands as we jogged back to the bench. "We can still get back in this game. Let's not quit out there."

A few guys tried to talk it up, but it was a sorry effort. I wondered if some members of the team were ready to quit. We had won our first game of the season, but since then the Icemen hadn't been able to do anything right. Joey Mehta said we were jinxed, and at times, I almost believed him.

After Greg Palazzo struck out and Joey popped to third, Nick looked at the dog, who was still sitting behind the bench sniffing at the air.

"Have you ever seen her before, Coach?" he asked.

"Nope," he replied. "But someone must own her. She's dirty, but she doesn't look hungry." He turned back to the action on the field. "Come on, Toby. Get a hit!"

No such luck. Toby Davis grounded to short and we had to head back onto the field. We were able to sneak in one run before the end of the game, though. I hit a single to lead off the seventh and then scored on a triple by Carl. We lost our fifth straight, 9-1.

Most of the guys left right after the game. I couldn't blame them. It's hard to hang out at the site of such a humiliating loss. A few of us stayed behind to play with the dog. We tossed a Frisbee, and the dog chased it and retrieved it, supporting my theory that she was part retriever. Her tail wagged so much when she barked that I thought she would wag it off. She definitely loved attention.

I was waiting for Ollie, whose team had a game on the other side of the park. Finally, I saw him pedaling his bike my way, his long legs pumping furiously.

"Don't tell me," Ollie said, as he skidded to a stop in front of me. "You lost again."

"How'd you know?" I asked. "Does it show on my face?"

"I ran into Joey Mehta," Ollie replied. "He's not a happy camper."

"No one is," I added. "Except her." I pointed to the dog, who was still playing with Nick and a couple of the others.

"That dog?" Ollie asked, laughing. "She stopped our game for a few minutes this afternoon until we ran her off."

"Well, you ran her straight to us," I said, frowning at Ollie. "But she's not so bad. I kind of feel sorry for her."

"Maybe that's a case for us," Ollie said thoughtfully. "Finding her owner."

Even though we hadn't had a case in a while, I thought Ollie was stretching it a bit. I mean, we weren't even sure the dog was lost. But I decided to keep my eyes open anyway.

I said good-bye to the guys and grabbed my bike. All the way home, I could not get that dog out of my mind. She seemed to love baseball as much as I do.

Δ   Δ   Δ

Two days later, the Icemen had another game. We were playing the Hawk Industry Hurricanes, and after two innings they were already blowing us away 3-0. Coach Roberts had started Chad Lewis in rightfield, so I was on the bench. As I watched the Hurricanes score yet another run, I felt something nudge me in the back.

"Hey, girl," I said, scratching the familiar dog behind

97

the ears. "Here to watch the game?" I asked. While I petted her, we finally got the third out and the team came back to the bench. Nick Klein spotted his pal right away.

"Hey!" he exclaimed. "You're back!"

Nick and a few other players came over to pet her. Then Coach Roberts started shouting orders.

"Get your minds back on the game, guys!" he barked out like a drill sergeant. I felt a little sorry for the coach. It must be tough to deal with a losing team. I wondered if the other coaches laughed at him like the other teams laughed at us. "We're not out of it, yet. Three runs are easy to make up! Russ," Coach called out, "you're up."

Russ Emrich led off with a pop-up straight at the pitcher. One out. Joey Mehta left the on-deck circle, and as he started up to the plate, he felt something tugging at his shoelace. It was the dog.

"Hey, girl," Joey said, pushing the dog's head away. "I'm up, let me go."

The more Joey tried to push her away, the closer the dog stood to him. He could not get free of her to go bat. Even a dog doesn't want to see our miserable batting performances, I thought. Pitiful.

"Hey, Joey," Nick called. "She's just playing. Pet her a little and maybe she'll let go."

Sure enough, once Joey rubbed the dog's nose, she stepped back. Joey went up to the plate.

The first pitch whizzed right up the middle of the plate and Joey didn't even twitch. Strike one. Then, on the next pitch, Joey made solid contact with a change-up. He slammed the ball down the leftfield line for a double. For the first time in weeks, our bench came alive.

"All right, Joey!"

"Way to hit!"

Ronnie Barnes stepped up to the plate.

"Hey, Ronnie! Pet the dog!" Joey called from second base.

Ronnie stopped and looked curiously at the dog, who was sitting in the on-deck circle, thumping her tail.

"Just pet her," Joey repeated. "She's good luck!"

"Do it, Ronnie," Greg Palazzo yelled from the bench. "It can't hurt." A couple of the other guys joined in, urging Ronnie to pet the dog and get on with the game.

Shrugging, Ronnie took a step toward the dog, who immediately ran over and sank her teeth into his shoelaces.

"Oh, man!" Ronnie yelled. "Let go! No!"

"Pet her," Joey hollered from second. "She'll let go."

As soon as Ronnie started stroking the dog's head, she let go of his shoelace and trotted back to her spot in the on-deck circle.

"She just about ripped my shoelace in half," Ronnie complained, examining the ragged laces.

"Just get up there, Ronnie," Coach Roberts growled, eyeing the umpire.

Finally, Ronnie stepped into the box. He sent the first pitch over the fence for a two-run homer.

"See ya!" I yelled, jumping to my feet and watching the ball fall a good 20 yards past the fence.

"Way to go, you lucky lady," Joey Mehta called, running over to give the wildly barking dog a big hug.

And that's how Lady got her name and became our good luck charm. Every guy on the team rubbed Lady's nose before he batted, and we started sending the ball all over the field. At the end of the game, we had racked up an unbelievable 13 runs to the Hurricanes' 4.

After the game, the whole team gathered around Lady.

"You sure brought us good luck today, Lady," Joey told her, petting Lady's nose. "Make sure you come to the next game, O.K.?"

"Yeah," Russ chimed in. "We don't want to lose our lucky charm."

This was a problem. No one knew who owned the dog, or even if she had an owner. And none of the players could take the dog home with him.

"What about you, Coach?" Nick finally asked.

"Yeah, Coach," Joey said, looking up from where he was petting Lady, who had just returned the Frisbee he had thrown. "If you take her in, she could be at every game."

Coach Roberts rolled his eyes, and then turned to Lady. She was off chasing the Frisbee again, wagging her tail with excitement. Don Roberts took off his cap and rubbed his forehead as if he was thinking over the situation.

"Tell you what, guys," he called. "Since there aren't any tags on her," Coach continued, taking a look at Lady's old, worn collar, "I'll take Lady home—for now! Then I'll call up the dog pound to see if anyone's looking for her, and I'll put an ad in the paper tomorrow. Is that O.K. with you guys?"

We all nodded our agreement, secretly hoping that her owners wouldn't really come for her.

"So," Coach Roberts went on to say, "if the owners don't come for her, you can be sure Lady will be at every game!" We all jumped around and cheered and Lady barked her approval. "Come on," the coach shouted above our voices, "let's go get free ice cream!"

We all cheered again and practically raced into town to Kreagle's Ice Cream Shop. Now that I knew Lady was going to be taken care of, I was definitely in the mood for a huge dish of chocolate fudge ice cream.

Δ   Δ   Δ

No one responded to the ad Coach Roberts put in the paper, so he kept bringing Lady to our games. The Roberts had bathed and brushed her until she looked fantastic. Her coat was shiny black, and her white patches shone like stadium floodlights.

Lady barked and jumped like a cheerleader when we rallied or made a good play on the field. Whenever we went to pet her, she would grab onto our shoelaces and wag her tail wildly. Joey, Nick and a few others were convinced that it was Lady who helped us win 12 out of our next 14 games. That gave us the division title with a record of 14-7. Next we would face the Lamar's Garage Pumpers for the league championship.

"We'll really need Lady for that one!" Joey said at our team meeting on the Monday after we had clinched our division. The Pumpers were 17-4 for the season, and most people claimed they were the best team in the league. "With our lucky mascot, the Icemen can do no wrong!"

"Yeah," Ronnie Barnes agreed. "We'll need all the luck Lady's got."

"Do you guys really believe that Lady is the reason you're winning?" Coach Roberts asked the team, astonished. "Just her luck?"

"It hasn't hurt," Greg Palazzo said, tossing a ball up and catching it in his mitt. "You have to admit that we've been winning ever since Lady showed up!"

"Well, boys," our coach said solemnly, "Lady is not the reason you've been winning."

"What do you mean?" Nick asked, knitting his brows.

"You didn't win anything before because you weren't working as a team," Coach corrected. "It just took a while for everything to come together. You're winning now because you have strong fundamentals and good teamwork. *That's* what wins ball games, not a good luck charm!"

The team was silent as Coach looked us over. "Now," he finally continued, "is Lady responsible for the way you hit and field and pitch?"

"No, she isn't," I said, standing and pushing my glasses up on my nose. "Coach is right, guys! All we have to do is keep playing the same way we have been. Nothing can stop the Icemen!"

"Yeah," Joey said, "and playing the same way means petting Lady for luck. She's the one thing that we have that the Pumpers don't."

"O.K., boys. That's enough," Coach Roberts said. "We have practices tomorrow, Wednesday and Thursday and a team meeting on Friday. Let's make the most of them."

Δ   Δ   Δ

Most of the team arrived early for practice on Tuesday afternoon, but Coach Roberts was late. When he finally showed up, we all rushed to the car to get our equipment and greet Lady, who usually jumped out of the car the minute Coach Roberts opened the door. But not this time.

"Hey, Coach," Joey called. "Where's Lady? Here, Lady!"

I expected Lady to jump out when her name was called, but she didn't. When we reached the car, Coach Roberts was sitting on the hood of his station wagon.

"Where's Lady, Coach?" Nick asked, repeating Joey's question.

After a long pause, the coach finally spoke."I've got some bad news for you, boys," the coach began, looking worried. "Mrs. Roberts and I think that Lady has run away."

There was a moment of shocked silence, and then everyone was suddenly talking all at once. Joey's voice, sounding tense and almost scared, cut through the noisy babble.

"Run away? She'd never do that!" he exclaimed. "She loved coming to practice and the games. She wouldn't just run away!"

"How did it happen, Coach?" I asked once Joey had quieted down. This was a case no one would have to ask me to take.

"We always put her out back on a rope at night," Coach began explaining. "We let her in when we're ready for bed.

But when my wife went to bring her in last night, Lady was gone. Somehow, the rope had gotten loose."

"Did you look for her?" I asked, switching from substitute rightfielder to Jack B. Quick, detective.

"Of course we looked for her!" Coach Roberts exclaimed, looking upset. "We drove around for over an hour last night, and again this morning. I even called the dog pound. I hope she'll show up there."

"Maybe she'll show up here!" Nick suggested. "You know how much she loves being around the team."

"If we can't find Lady," Joey stated, "we won't have a chance against the Pumpers!" At this, a lot of my teammates started talking loudly again.

"Didn't any of you hear what I said yesterday?" Coach asked, raising his voice above all of ours. "Lady is not the reason you've been winning!" he said firmly. "Of course, if you don't think you'll win without Lady, then you probably won't. But I *know* you're good enough to beat the Pumpers—with or without Lady."

Everyone was silent after this. Most of the team started glancing around the ballfield. They seemed to be looking for Lady, as if she would show up at any second. I was busy planning my strategy for *The Case of the Lucky Lady*.

"Hey! Jack's a detective," Greg said, breaking the silence. "He can find her!"

"Yeah, how about it, Jack?" Joey added. "Do you think you can find Lady?"

"Don't worry, guys," I said to the team. "I'm already on the case."

When practice ended, I shot home like a bullet fired out of a gun barrel. Before I even caught my breath, I called Ollie and our other associate, Nina Chin, and asked them to come over as soon as possible.

I grabbed a quick shower and then opened a computer file for the case. When my associates arrived, I was staring at the computer screen.

"Time to go to work," I told Nina and Ollie. "This case has to be solved by Friday. We need Lady for Saturday's game, and we can't find her anywhere."

"Lady's missing?" Nina asked in disbelief.

I told Nina and Ollie what Coach Roberts had told us. I had been telling Nina about our "good luck charm" just the day before. "The team is really concerned about Lady, and I said I'd find her," I added, pushing my glasses up on my nose and looking at each of my associates in turn.

"Well, do you think she's lost, or do you think someone took her?" Ollie asked. That was the question that had been on my mind all day.

"Good point," Nina added. "Perhaps somebody doesn't want you guys to win that game."

"Well, Lady is a loyal dog," I began, considering the suggestion. "She seemed to be happy with her new home with the Roberts, and she loved coming to the park for our practices and games. It doesn't make sense that she would just run away unless she followed some other dog. My guess is that someone took her."

"We should put an ad in the paper anyway," Nina pointed out. "There's still a chance that she did run away."

"That sounds like a good idea," I said, nodding.

"We should also make fliers to put up in grocery stores and the post office," Ollie suggested, grabbing a pad and pen. He can draw pretty well and he did a good likeness of Lady. The flier was half-drawn before he had finished his sentence.

"Doesn't your coach live over on Quaker Street?" Nina asked. I nodded, staring at my computer screen.

"Bobby Ransom lives there, too," Nina stated.

"Isn't he the captain of the Pumpers?" Ollie asked us.

"You bet he is!" I said, slamming my fist on the computer table. "We've been listening to him brag all summer. If his team loses the championship, he won't be able to show his face when school starts next week. I wonder if *he* took Lady."

"That would fall right in with my theory," Nina pointed out. I keyed in Bobby Ransom's name on top of the suspect list. After that, Nina and I typed up our ad for the paper while Ollie finished the flier.

Nina offered to make copies of the flier at the library and to drop off the ad. Ollie and I headed for Quaker Street. Ollie walked down the block and I went to talk with Bobby Ransom. Fortunately, he was home.

"Well, well," Bobby sneered as soon as he answered the door. "Jack B. Quick. So-so detective, lousy ball player. What's up?"

Being the mature, businesslike detective that I am, I decided to ignore the remark about my baseball prowess. Not to mention that Bobby *is* Ollie's size.

"Do you mind if I talk to you for a second?" I asked.

"Hope you don't want to make any bets for Saturday," he said, laughing. "You'd be a sure loser!"

"No. No bets," I informed him.

"Hmm, too bad, Quick," he said, pretending to be disappointed. "I could have made some money off of you."

"You haven't seen a black dog with white patches running around the neighborhood, have you?" I asked, getting down to business. "It belongs to our coach, Don Roberts."

"You mean that old mutt who's always hanging around your games?" Bobby asked, a bit nastily.

"Yes. She's disappeared," I informed him. "Coach thinks she ran away, but I'm not so sure."

"That mutt's your team mascot, isn't she?" Bobby asked, still laughing. "And I've heard she's your good luck charm, too."

"So you haven't seen her?" I asked, getting back to my original question.

"No," he said. "I've been too busy getting ready to beat you on Saturday."

"Do you mind if I have a glass of water?" I asked. I wanted to check out his kitchen for clues, and I really was as dry as a bone. Bobby led me to the kitchen and handed me a glass of ice water. While I was drinking it, I noticed a large bag of dog food in the corner next to the sink.

"Do you have a dog, Bobby?" I asked him.

"No. Both of my parents work," he explained. "They keep saying it wouldn't be fair to leave a dog alone in the house all day. I'll talk them into it someday, though."

"Oh, well," I said, as he walked me to the front door. "If you see our mascot, let me know, will you?"

"Sure. But remember, Quick," he called as I climbed on my bike. "No good luck charm is going to save you on Saturday! We'll beat you by at least five runs."

I rode off without answering. Ollie was waiting for me on the corner.

"I may be on to something, Ollie," I said as we rode home.

"You think Bobby stole Lady?" he asked.

"He said he didn't have a dog, but there was a bag of dog food in his kitchen," I explained.

"But would he keep a dog only two doors away from its home?" Ollie questioned.

"That's true," I replied. Ollie *did* have a point. "Maybe he's keeping Lady somewhere else."

"How would we find out?" Ollie asked.

"I think we should come back later and do a little spy work," I said. "Don't you?" Ollie just smiled—he loves to spy.

Nina arrived at my house shortly after Ollie and I did. She had put up signs in about a dozen different places, and had placed our ad with the *Belleville Gazette*. Now we were ready to rock and roll.

Δ   Δ   Δ

The next day, before practice, I met up with Ollie and Nina. I knew that the Pumpers had an early practice that day, so we made a surprise visit to the Ransom house. Mrs.

Ransom answered the door. I asked for Bobby.

"He isn't home," she replied. "He has an early practice this morning."

"Well, have you seen a black dog with white patches running around the neighborhood?" I asked.

"No, I haven't," she answered. "Is that the Roberts' new dog? Actually, I haven't seen her for a few days."

"Did she ever come over to play with your dog?" I asked.

"We don't have a dog," she replied.

So, what was up with the dog food in her kitchen, I wondered.

"Thanks for your help, Mrs. Ransom," I said, and turned to leave. Just at that moment, we all heard a yelp come from inside the house.

"No dog, huh, Jack?" Ollie whispered to me with a smirk.

"Oh, shush, Muffin!" Mrs. Ransom admonished as a white miniature poodle ran up to the screen door.

"I thought you didn't have a dog," Nina commented accusingly.

"We don't," Mrs. Ransom insisted. "Muffin is my sister's dog. We're dog-sitting for a few days."

We all rode home in silence. Our Number 1 clue and suspect had been washed down the drain by a yapping poodle named Muffin. I asked Nina to come by my practice and keep her eyes open, just in case. Ollie had his own practice to go to. His team was in the playoffs as well.

At home, I climbed the staircase to my room and

entered all of this disappointing information into the computer. Wherever Lady was, I hoped she was safe and that we could find her by Saturday.

Δ   Δ   Δ

Wednesday's practice was just as morose as Tuesday's had been. Most of my teammates were still talking about Lady and how they missed her. Of course, they also asked how I was doing on the case. I didn't have the heart to tell them that my associates and I were back to square one. Instead, I told them that we were following up a lead, but that I couldn't tell them anything about it for security reasons. When I finished talking, the boys looked a little bit more confident. I noticed that Coach Roberts gave me a long look before he started practice.

"Lady's a smart dog," Coach Roberts told us. "Look how she found her way here. I'm sure that wherever she is, someone is taking good care of her. Besides," he went on, "you've got Jack on the case, and my wife and I are still looking for her. Now let's concentrate on baseball and get this practice going."

We all tried our best, but it was difficult. Lady's disappearance was hanging over us like a dark storm cloud. I was worrying about how this case would turn out. I had no leads and no more suspects. There hadn't been any calls about the lost dog posters that Nina had put up. I hoped the ad in the *Belleville Gazette* would prove worthwhile.

There were 10 or 15 kids hanging out by the bleachers and watching our practice. Among them was Nina, doing her detective work. I saw her talking to a few of the spectators. "I might be on to something," she said after practice was over. "You know Bill Franklin?"

"Yes," I replied. "I've traded baseball cards with him before. He's got a great collection."

"Well, I was eavesdropping while Bill bet part of his collection on Lamar's Garage Pumpers," Nina said.

"Wow," I said. "If he loses that bet, he'll have to practically start from scratch. Who did he make the bet with?"

"Some guy named Dave Van Dorn," Nina told me. "I didn't recognize him, so I had to ask someone what his name was."

"How did Bill act when he made the bet?" I asked.

"It was like he knew the Pumpers would win," Nina explained. "He said that the Icemen would melt in the first inning. He couldn't have been more confident if he had had a written guarantee."

"This could be the break that we've been waiting for," I informed Nina. "Let me talk to the team before they all leave."

It turned out that three of the guys knew Bill Franklin pretty well. Greg Palazzo told me that he had been arguing with Bill all summer about which team was better.

"It just so happens," I said to Nina as we rode away from the field, "that Bill's best friend is Ed O'Reilly. He's pitching for the Pumpers on Saturday!"

"I see," Nina said, absorbing this information.

"Dave Van Dorn is a cousin of Nick Klein, our leftfielder," I went on. "He's been a big fan of ours ever since

Lady brought us that winning streak. He bet a basketball and a brand-new hockey stick against some of the best cards in Bill's collection."

"I wonder," Nina said as we stopped at a light. "Why was Bill so sure you guys would lose to the Pumpers?"

We went over to my house and called Ollie. I wanted him to get as much info on Bill Franklin as possible.

There were two messages on our answering machine about the fliers. Both calls were about stray black dogs that had been taken in within the past two days.

An older woman named Mrs. Quigley answered the door at the first house. A huge black Newfoundland jumped through the doorway as soon as the door was open, pinning me to the porch and licking my face off.

"No, this isn't Lady," I gasped under the weight of the monstrous dog.

"Oh, dear," Mrs. Quigley said, obviously disappointed. "I was so hoping it was yours."

"So were we," Nina replied, giggling at my predicament. I was too busy trying to get out from under this enormous Newfoundland to even scowl at her.

Finally, the dog got off of me. Mrs. Quigley apologized for its behavior. We thanked her for calling us and went on.

At the next house, a tiny little terrier came yipping to the door. It wasn't our Lady, but I was thankful it wasn't another 150-pound monster of a dog. When we got back to my house, Ollie was shooting hoops in my driveway.

"Pay dirt, boss," he said, as Nina and I dismounted from our bikes. "Maybe," he added quietly, with a frown.

"Maybe?" I asked, frustrated with this case. "What's the catch?"

"Well," Ollie began. "I'm not sure if this will lead to anything, but—" Ollie paused. I knew he was making sure he had my attention. "Word is that our friend, Bill Franklin, got a dog yesterday."

Ollie definitely had my attention now. "A dog? Yesterday?" I asked.

"Yep. I talked to a Melissa Johnson—she's Bill's neighbor," Ollie informed us. "She said he'd been talking about his new dog all day."

"What kind? What color?" I asked Ollie impatiently.

"She wasn't sure," Ollie replied. "That's why I said maybe."

"I knew there was a catch," I muttered, pushing my glasses back up on my nose.

In seconds, we were all biking across town—again. But no one was home at the Franklins'. They must have taken the dog with them, too, because it didn't bark when we rang the doorbell. We waited about half an hour, sitting under a shady tree in the yard, but no one showed.

"I have to get going," I said at last. "Dad will be mad if I'm late—detective work or not."

When I said this, it seemed as if all three of our stomachs growled with hunger, so we pedaled home.

The next day was Thursday—our last team practice. All I had was one shaky lead. Of course, sometimes, that's all a good detective needs to solve a case. But if the Franklins' dog wasn't Lady, then I was at another dead end.

That night I didn't sleep too well, though I should have. I was exhausted from practice and riding around town all day. But when a case has this many bad leads, I can't help thinking about it. It took a long time for me to fall asleep.

Δ   Δ   Δ

I was exhausted at practice, and a bunch of my teammates seemed to feel the same way. A couple of them even expressed doubts about my abilities as a detective.

When practice had ended, some guy suddenly limped over to the coach and shook hands. I noticed that he had some pretty bad scars on his right leg.

"Guys," the coach called to all of us, "I'd like you to meet my brother, Terry. I asked him to come here because I have a quitting team on my hands."

We all looked at each other, then at the ground. Coach Roberts went on. "Terry isn't here to give you guys a speech or anything like that. I just want you to take a good look at him." A few of us, myself included, looked up sheepishly.

"A few years ago, Terry was in a car accident. His injuries were so severe that the doctors didn't expect him to live—but he hung in there. Then they said that he would never walk. He didn't quit then, either. When he started walking around, the doctors told Terry that he would always have to wear a leg brace. See for yourself."

We all looked at Terry's legs. He was wearing shorts, and there was obviously no brace on his leg.

"Terry's next goal," Coach Roberts went on, "is to run a marathon. He's already running 10 miles a day, and he thinks he'll be ready for the marathon in a year or so. Even

114

though that's more than 26 grueling miles, I wouldn't bet against him. If you guys have even half the guts that Terry has, you could beat the Pumpers without any good luck charm."

Then Terry told us about all the time he had spent in physical therapy and how many operations had been performed on his leg. There were times, he told us, that he had begun to doubt whether he would make it, but he had been determined to pull himself through. "If you want something bad enough," Terry told us before he left, "you can get it."

What I wanted was to find Lady. Ollie showed up at the field just as we were saying good-bye to Terry, and the two of us zoomed off to Bill Franklin's house. Nina was paying a visit to the dog pound.

Bill's mother answered the door and invited us in for some lemonade. We accepted without any hesitation. While inside, though, we found no sign of a dog.

"I heard you just got a dog about two days ago," I mentioned to Mrs. Franklin.

"Yes," Mrs. Franklin chirped with a big smile. "He's adorable!" She picked up an envelope full of photographs from the counter. She put it down in front of Ollie and me and pulled out picture after picture of a black Labrador puppy. "His name is Pepper. Billy has him at the park right now."

"Oh, well," I said, standing up. "We'd better be going, Mrs. Franklin. Thanks for the lemonade, and good luck with your new dog."

Ollie and I rode back to my house, and shot hoops in

my driveway. We didn't even notice when Nina rode up behind us.

"Any luck?" she asked hopefully.

Ollie shook his head.

"Me neither," she stated with a frown. "I checked the dog pound, the animal rescue shelter and even a bunch of pet shops," she sighed. "No one knew a thing about Lady. The dog warden wasn't even looking for her!"

"We're getting nowhere fast with this case," Ollie complained.

"Well," I said, letting out a sigh myself. "I just hope we don't strike out on Saturday. Maybe Terry Roberts will have some influence on the guys."

"Who's he?" Nina asked.

I told her.

"Wow!" Nina exclaimed. "He must be quite a guy!"

"He sure is," I told her. "He's training for a marathon. He runs 10 miles every day."

"Awesome!" Ollie the athlete claimed. Who wouldn't be impressed?

After my associates had left, I sat down in front of the computer to add the day's events to the *Lucky Lady* file. What I had on the screen looked like a dead-end case.

Even if Lady had run away, she wouldn't have just disappeared. She would look for people—she loves attention. Lady must have been dognapped.

Then I remembered something Nina had said. If Coach Roberts had called the dog pound when he found out that Lady was missing, the dog warden should have been looking for Lady. But Nina had said that the warden didn't know anything about her. That was odd. I would have to check into that myself—as soon as possible.

Δ   Δ   Δ

Mr. Jeffords, the dog warden, was in his office at the Belleville Pound.

"I'm looking for a lost dog," I told him. "And I didn't see her in any of the pens." I then went on to explain all about Lady, adding that Coach Roberts had called in to report that she was missing.

"Roberts? I don't recall the name," Mr. Jeffords said blankly. "I'll check my records." He stood up and opened his filing cabinet. "Nope," he said, after flipping through a number of folders. "I have no record of a Roberts or a description of the dog. He may have spoken to one of my assistants, and they might have forgotten to file it properly. That has happened before."

"Well, here," I said, handing him one of the fliers Ollie had drawn. "This should make things easier for you."

"Indeed it does," he claimed, as he pinned it up above his desk. "If anything turns up, I'll let you know right away."

"Thanks a lot!" I said, rushing out the door. According to my watch, I only had about 10 minutes to make the team meeting on time.

When I arrived at the field, I was welcomed as I had expected to be welcomed—with questions about Lady.

"I haven't found her yet, guys," I admitted to the team. "So far, all of my leads have been dead ends."

"What now?" Joey asked. "The game is tomorrow."

"I'm still looking," I informed everybody. "I never quit on a case. But either way, we have to try and win—with or without Lady."

"We'll never do it without Lady," Joey said bitterly. I couldn't believe how much some members of the team were depending on a dog.

"Coach is right," I suddenly said. "We can't depend on Lady to help us win the game. What if she's not there?" I paused. "We might as well quit right now. I don't think I'm going to find Lady before the game tomorrow. But I'm not going to quit looking for her, so why should we give up on winning? We should win this game *for* Lady! We owe it to her!"

"Come on, guys," Ronnie added. "Jack's got a point. We can still play even if Lady's not there."

"She helped us out of our slump," Nick said, jumping into the pep rally I had started. "But we're the ones who hit the ball and made the plays that got us to the championship."

"O.K., guys," Coach Roberts called. I had no idea how long he and his brother had been standing there, but I'm sure they had heard enough. "Let's get this meeting going."

We went over the starting lineup, and we talked a lot about Lamar's Garage Pumpers and how we should approach their game. "So," Coach Roberts concluded, "if we make all the right plays, and we don't beat ourselves, we can play with them. And if we can do that, we've got a chance to win."

With that, he dismissed the team and headed off for his car. I chased after him, wanting to inform him of my progress with the case and of what I had told the team earlier.

While I was talking to Coach and Terry, I noticed something about Terry's bad leg. "Uh, Coach?" I asked, in the middle of my report. "Can we go someplace and talk—privately?"

"How about my car?" Terry suggested.

"Great," I told them, and we headed for his station wagon.

Δ   Δ   Δ

Saturday morning was perfect for a baseball game. It was sunny, but not too hot, and the humidity was low. The stands were packed with spectators, as usual. The Summer League Baseball Championship games are always a big deal in Belleville.

Just before the game started, I went to talk with Ollie and Nina, who were sitting right behind our bench, about the case.

"I've got the jitters," I told them, pushing my glasses up. Coach Roberts had surprised me yesterday when he announced that I was to start in rightfield today.

"You'll get used to it," Ollie, the old pro, said.

"How do you feel about . . . " Nina started to ask, but then paused and looked around. "Well, you know."

"I talked with the coach," I answered. "I agreed to play it his way a little longer. I think it's the right thing to do. But I don't think a lot of my teammates will agree. I guess we'll have to wait until after the game."

"Go get 'em, Jack!" Ollie called as I ran to the bench.

The coin toss made us the home team, but things didn't

start off too well. When we got to bat in the bottom of the first inning, we were already down 2-0.

"I'd love to see Lady here now," Ronnie Barnes sighed.

"The hits are in your bats!" the coach snapped. He glowered at us, sitting on the bench. "Concentrate on the game, boys!"

In the third inning, I finally got up to bat. Unfortunately, I grounded out to the shortstop. By then it was 3-0, courtesy of a Bobby Ransom homer. In the fourth inning, though, things started to change in our favor.

Joey, at the top of the order, led off with a single to center. Then Nick banged a single to left, bringing our bench to life. We needed the runs badly, and we cheered like crazy. Russ Emrich ran the count to 2-2, then popped out to deep right. Joey, however, tagged up and made it to third, giving us runners on first and third.

Greg Palazzo batted Joey in with a single to right, but that was where our rally ended. At least we were on the scoreboard now, 3-1.

I led off in the fifth inning and walked. Chad Lewis was up next, and Coach Roberts signaled me to steal. I'm not much of a hitter, but keeping up with Ollie has made me pretty fast on my feet.

Watching Ed O'Reilly, the Pumper pitcher, like a hawk, I got a good lead and took off as soon as he started to the plate. The catcher's throw was a good one, but I slid in safely using the hook slide Ollie had taught me. When I got up to dust myself off, I noticed Ollie and Nina waving from the stands. I waved back enthusiastically.

"Stay alert!" Coach Roberts called from the bench. I quickly turned my attention back to the game. Chad hit a bouncer to sacrifice me to third.

Toby Davis looped one over the shortstop for a single, batting me in for another run. Joey was up next and struck out, but Nick slammed a double, pushing Toby home to tie the game. Russ then singled, and Nick slid home, giving us the lead, 4-3. At this point, we were so psyched that we had all but forgotten about Lady.

In the next inning, the Pumpers took the lead, getting three runs off Kenny. We got one back, and at the bottom of the sixth, the score was 6-5. Going into our final at-bat, we were still behind by one run, and almost at the top of our batting order.

Before Toby went to the plate, Coach Roberts called us in for a huddle. "Listen, you guys. You can still do it," he said, encouraging us. "There's no reason why you shouldn't feel confident now. O'Reilly is getting tired out there on the mound. You've shown the Pumpers that you're every bit as good as they are, and Lady isn't even here! Now, let's go out and win this game!"

Everyone let out a shout, and Toby grabbed his bat to lead it off. He hit the ball sharply, but the shortstop caught it on one hop and threw him out easily.

As Joey made his way to the plate, he turned to the bench. "Let's do this for Lady!" he called. And after two balls, Joey slapped a base hit to rightfield, bringing up Nick Klein.

Nick took the first pitch and sent it deep into left

centerfield, past a diving Bobby Ransom. Joey was already rounding third by the time the ball was on its way back to the infield. Nick held up at second, but Joey had brought in the tying run. Our bench went crazy.

With one out, Russ Emrich stepped up to the plate. Russ blasted the first pitch into deep center. It should have been over the fence, for sure. But Bobby Ransom, slamming into the fence, caught the ball at the last minute, stealing Russ' home run. Still, Nick had tagged-up and went to third.

Greg Palazzo came up to the plate. He didn't show it, but he must have been nervous. The game was riding on him—otherwise we would have to go into extra innings.

I had my fingers crossed, and I even tried crossing my toes. Greg worked it up to a full count. O'Reilly's pitch was a high fastball. Greg went after it, hitting a bouncer up the gap between short and third.

Greg sprinted to first. Nick rocketed toward home. The shortstop made a diving stop and had to jump up before he could throw. His throw was as fast as O'Reilly's fastball was. But the throw was high, and the catcher had to go up for it. And Nick slid under him for the winning run.

Everyone went berserk. I had seen celebrations like this before, but I had never been part of one. It was great—even being on the bottom of the pile. But before we began to un-pile ourselves, I was already thinking about the surprise that was still to come.

When things had finally settled down, Coach Roberts assembled us all. "You guys really pulled together out there today," he praised us. "I always knew that you would. But I had to do something to make sure you would. I just hope you'll all understand why I did it."

The whole team looked puzzled. I was sure no one knew what he was talking about.

"Last Monday," he explained, "I told you that Lady had disappeared. You asked Jack to find her." He paused. "Well, you had a first-rate detective on the case."

All the guys glued their eyes on me. They knew it was Lady we were talking about, but they still had no idea why.

"You see," Coach Roberts went on, "Jack solved the case yesterday. But I asked him not to tell you about it," he said. He stopped then, and waved his hand to Terry. Terry had just pulled his car up behind the backstop.

Then Terry opened the door and stepped out. "LADY!" everyone shouted at once. She jumped out of the car right behind Terry, almost knocking him over as she bounded toward us.

In seconds, we were celebrating all over again. It was almost impossible to get a hand on Lady as we all crowded around her. We ended up taking turns and hugging her.

"What exactly happened to Lady?" Ronnie finally asked.

"Well," I started, "it was a tough case. All of my leads went nowhere. I had nothing but dead ends in front of me. Since it seemed unlikely that Lady would just run away, I assumed that she had been dognapped.

"After two-and-a-half days of getting nowhere, my partners, Ollie and Nina, and I were ready to give up. But then we discovered that Mr. Jeffords, the dog warden, had no report on Lady, even though Coach had said that he had reported her missing.

"Then," I continued with my debriefing on the case, "I noticed Terry's shoelaces. They were torn and ragged—as if someone had been chewing on them."

"Just like Lady used to do to us!" Joey blurted out.

"Exactly," I agreed. "That's when I confronted Coach."

"Coach took Lady?" Nick said in disbelief.

"Yes," Coach Roberts said, taking over. "I took her to my brother's house. I felt you boys were depending too much on Lady to help you win the championship. I was afraid that if you fell behind, you'd figure Lady's luck ran out and give up. It was a tough decision, but I had to do it to make you guys a real team."

"I'm just glad she's back," Joey said, hugging Lady.

My voice was hoarse from all the cheering I had done that day, but I was still able to get out my favorite words, "Case closed!"